Guardian Angel

Guardian Angel

Peter Walsh

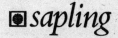

First published in the UK in 1996 by Sapling, an imprint of
Boxtree Limited, Broadwall House, 21 Broadwall London SE1 9PL

Published by arrangement with The Berkley Publishing Group,
a division of The Putnam Berkley Group, Inc., New York

ISBN: 0 7522 2206 6

Typeset by SX Composing DTP, Rayleigh, Essex
Printed and bound in Great Britain

A catalogue record is available from the British Library

Chapter 1

It's summer in my town. I'm nearly eighteen and life couldn't get any better.

I don't remember it ever being this hot. It's so hot the roads are melting, the edge of the asphalt turning into a black wax. There's no wind. I sit in my room at the top of the house, with all the windows open. I can hear kids playing out in the street, the odd car cruising past. My town is quiet. Not much happens. It's a commuter town, a high street with the usual chain-stores, one cinema, a few thousand people in neat semi-detached houses. My mother moved here from London when I was eleven years old. She wanted to get away from the noise and the crowds of the city. From the back of our house all you can see are fields and trees.

A few months ago this place was driving me crazy. Everyone knows each other, nothing new ever happens. I wanted to get out. My mother was worried I might fail all the exams I was taking at school because she knew I was unhappy but I was working harder than ever. Good grades were my ticket out. Some of my friends are planning to study in London at college. If I do well I could move down there with them, rent some rooms in a house maybe.

The exams are over. They finished last week. I think I've done all right but that's not why I'm feeling so good. The reason why life has improved so dramatically is much wilder than that. I'm seeing a girl. I'm seeing Sarah, the most beautiful girl I've ever known.

I've been into her for a long time but she never seemed interested in me. At school she went out with guys from the upper years, the good-looking 'football star' types. She always had a gang around her. We talked now and again but she was out of reach, I didn't think I had a chance. Then two weeks ago I went to a party and she was there. She looked better than ever, as though there was a halo around her or something. We started talking and I ended up walking her home. I've been alone with her like that a few times and never had the courage to say anything but that evening I decided it was make or break. I was going to be daring. It still feels like I was in a trance, I stopped caring, just leaned forward and kissed her on the lips, put my fingers deep into her hair. We stayed out for another hour. She said she wanted to see me.

We were both working for the exams but I've managed to see her almost every day. Yesterday she met me on the high street and said she was taking me somewhere special. We walked over towards the station. There are some new development blocks there, expensive flats and shops. She took me into a new block of flats, cream carpets and lots of glass. Then she produced a key and we went into a large apartment, a palatial suite compared to my house. We sat down on a huge sofa and she told me the place belonged to her father's company. They use it for meetings and for visiting businessmen. She told me that we could use it in the afternoons when she knew there'd be no one there. I just stared at her and she smiled.

We didn't do anything that afternoon, just watched some videos and kissed. I felt very mature, sitting there, holding on to her.

Life is good at the moment. I've got all summer with Sarah and I can take my time before making a decision about college. I just want to relax and hang out with her.

I'm going over to see her now. I shut the windows and head down to the kitchen. My mother won't be back for an hour or two so I pull the back door shut and double-lock it. Then I cut through the garden and into the woods. It's a short cut over to Sarah's house.

When I was a kid the woods used to scare me. Sometimes I'd be in our back garden and I'd stare out into it and think I could see dark shapes among the trees, figures moving in the twilight shadows.

3

Here the town development ends, you step into a world that hasn't changed for thousands of years. As I got older I learnt all the trails and paths, climbed the trees and explored. The fear gradually went away.

I walk through to a clearing then I have to take a path that leads past the monument and down to Sarah's street. The woods are cool and the sun's not too bright, I can see clouds of insects in the air. After a few minutes I get to the monument. It's an old crumbling Victorian arch, built so long ago everyone's forgotten what it was put there for. It's made of grey stone, covered in graffiti, about as tall as a house. There are four columns holding up a narrow platform, some writing along the top in Latin. I sit down on one of the wide base stones and rest for a moment. Even though it's cool the air is heavy and I'm sweating. Then I hear some movement in the bushes behind the monument and I flick my head around.

At first I think I'm a kid again and I'm staring at some kind of wood demon or wild animal. It's a figure, a boy, just a few feet away from me, running in my direction, a blur of motion. His face is so badly scarred on one side the skin looks molten, thick purple tissue from the chin to the hairline. His clothes are all torn and through a gash in his jeans I can see blood flowing down his leg. He tears past me but I catch sight of his eyes. They are full of panic, he's terrified. I stand up, about to call

4

after him, but he's in the undergrowth, pushing through into the trees.

And after the prey comes the first of the pack. Sweating and puffing, Luke Fisher stamps into the clearing and stares at me. He coughs and spits, then he wipes the sweat from his forehead.

'You see him?'

'Who?'

'The freak. Matthew.'

I say nothing. Some of Luke's ragged team are emerging from the bushes, brushing the dust and dirt from their clothes, moving off deeper into the wood.

'We've chased him all the way over here from my street. The guy can run.'

'What's he done?'

Luke doesn't answer me. He sits down on the monument base, pulls out a cigarette, lights it and takes a long pull.

Luke left school a year ago. I see him now and again, on the street, out at a party. He's wild. You don't mess around with Luke. He was suspended from school a few times, for fighting. He's tall and very thin, powerful, even though a few years of smoking and drinking have slowed him down a bit. I'm not small myself and because of this he's never bothered me. I'm an unknown quantity for Luke and I've always kept it like that, staying out of his way without actually backing down to him. I just want an easy life. There was always a lot of debate

5

at school about how it would turn out if we ever did fight but I was happy to avoid the outcome myself.

'Where'd he go?'

This time he wants an answer.

'I don't know. He wasn't exactly hanging around.'

'Don't stick your nose into this, Robbie.'

'I'm not doing. He ran into the bushes. I don't know which way he went.'

'All right.'

There's a shout from out in the trees. One of the gang is yelling for the others. Luke waves his arm and they rush out of the clearing, after the boy with the scars on his face.

Luke wouldn't be too bad if he wasn't so dumb. He operates on basic logic. I stand up and start walking. I can hear their shouts off in the woods.

I have to walk down a hill to come out at Sarah's street. On the left side of the hill there is a deep cut with high banks of earth. I glance through the trees that border the path I'm on and I can see Matthew standing alone in the bottom of the cut. He's staring up at the banks above him. Luke and his team are up on the top, silent, watching him. I stop walking. I should just carry on, I know, but I can't. I'm motionless, hidden in the trees.

'Hey, freak.'

Luke doesn't even shout. It's almost a whisper. The wood is so quiet I can hear Matthew panting.

6

He's covered in sweat, exhausted.

'Hey, burn boy, you coming up here or am I coming down there? Either way I'm gonna break every bone in your body, you hear me?'

Matthew doesn't reply. He's looking around, trying to see a way out.

'Benny. Go down and get him.'

One of the gang starts sliding down the dry earth bank to the base of the cut. He has to move slowly to avoid falling. Matthew is desperate now, he's wringing his hands, pacing in the small space left to him.

I could step through the trees and down into the cut. Benny wouldn't move on me. Luke would have to come down and do it and that might be enough time for Matthew to get out and get away, to reach the town and the streets and other people. But it's not my business. I don't know why I stay here, watching. I can't help him.

Benny's almost at the bottom. In a few more seconds he'll be shoving Matthew up the incline to take his beating. The blood's pounding in my head, a rush from my heart. I should do something but it would be mad to get involved. I want to know what Matthew's done. Why does Luke want to hurt him?

I look down and Matthew's staring up at me. He can't see through the trees but maybe he saw a shape, a movement I made unwittingly. He's looking directly at me. Benny's almost on him. Matthew throws himself up the steep bank, desperate to get out. He makes it a few feet then slides back down but he won't give in. I can hear Luke and the others laughing. Matthew's in a cloud of dust, scrabbling his way up the side. Suddenly the laughter stops. Matthew's half-way up. All his concentration is focused on making it up the side of that hill, he's grabbing on to roots and clumps of earth, like an insect, dragging himself up. Then he's just below me, a hand's reach away, I could lean forward and lift him out.

But I don't move. I stare into his face and let him break his nails and shred his fingers climbing out of the pit. He collapses on the ground, lifts himself up and runs past me and back into the wood.

Luke is shouting, trying to get them all moving, but they have no enthusiasm left for the chase.

'We'll catch up with him later.'

'I want him now.'

'Later, Luke.'

And I drop back into the bushes, unseen. I feel sick and hot, sit down in the grass. I should have helped him.

My father used to say you should watch out for yourself and stay out of other people's business. He runs his own company, in London. I don't think he ever made as much money as he wanted to but he's wealthy compared to most of the people in my town. He drives a Mercedes and lives with his girl-friend in a two-floor flat in West London. He

8

taught me to look after myself. I remember my parents rowing over some boxing-gloves he bought me once. That was on one of his visits, turning up on my birthday smelling of brandy, tobacco and aftershave, his girlfriend waiting out in the car. I hated him for a while but we get on all right now. I haven't told him I might be coming down to London to get a job for a year before going to Uni. He'd give me money, he might even let me stay at his flat. I go down there for weekends now and again. But I find it hard to talk with him. He doesn't listen. He hears what he wants. And I don't want my mother thinking I'm envious of his life, that I want to be just like him. That would upset her.

I'm amazed my parents ever got together. My mother is his opposite. I was too young in London to remember much of their relationship but she was unhappy, she wanted to get out. There are fragments in my memory, arguments and tears, the tension between them contained in an image, her sobbing in the kitchen, him staying out late, bringing loud friends back for dinner. When we moved out here she came to a new job, a new set of friends. She was smiling again. She teaches in the town primary school. I was old enough to avoid going there. I went straight into the comprehensive.

My mother cares about people. She's the type of person who crosses the street to help out if she sees someone in distress. Perhaps it was her influence that made me stop in the bushes, makes me feel guilty now for not helping Matthew. She would have gone down there with him, stood by his side. But she has never seen Luke standing over a kid, kicking him in the side, lifting his head and crashing his fist into the face, blood spattered, screaming. I've seen his eyes. Luke enjoys it. The only power and identity he has are provided by his violence. He has a reputation. People fear him and he thinks that fear is the same as respect. One day Luke will find out that no one respects him, that he's nothing. Violence is the last desperate alternative for Luke. He can't ride on it for ever, it'll bring him down eventually.

But I don't know when that day will come.

I didn't act. It was my father holding me back from helping. He would have left it, let Matthew fight his own battles. I know my father's not a coward. He just doesn't see the point in getting involved, in wasting his energy. Sometimes you try to help and it backfires, that would be his view. I think he's selfish as well. He's preoccupied with his own life and the struggles with the business. He didn't try to hold it together with my mother. The girlfriend came along very quickly after the separation. Too quickly, in my opinion. But I can't put my hesitation down to my parents. I was scared. I don't know how it would go if I fought Luke. It could go either way. Was it worth finding out just for Matthew?

Matthew's in my year at school. I've never really spoken with him, he's a loner, keeps to himself. No one hangs out with him. Matthew is an expert in hiding himself from the attention of others. When we come into a class he will find the desk at the back, in the corner, as far away from the other kids as he can get. He arrives at school a few minutes late in the morning and leaves as soon as we finish, never waits around to talk. I don't know if he's got anyone to talk to anyway. I haven't thought about him much before. He doesn't want to be noticed. His face is enough to shock. He tries to limit this by keeping his presence concealed.

His face is terribly scarred. The first time you see it is enough to make you feel blessed. Most people react with sympathy for a while, then they drift away from him, unconsciously avoid him, position themselves so they don't have to see him, don't have to deal with him. I can't imagine what Matthew's world is like. He lives with his mother down in the south of town. There are a few streets of council places there, tidy, pink brick houses. Some of the kids from school followed him down there once. They wanted to see where he lived. I think it was a bet they had with each other or something. Maybe they had nothing else to do but torment him, tracking him to his home, shouting taunts and insults. Matthew went into his house and they stood outside chatting. Then his mother came running out and started shouting at them.

They ran off. Ryan, a good friend of mine, heard the whole story from them. They told him that she looked crazy, wild hair, clothes all over the place.

It's always been easy not to think too much about Matthew. He never asks for anything or challenges anyone, never interacts. He doesn't want to be noticed. I see him on the high street occasionally. He hurries past, staring at the paving-stones, twisting his head slightly so it's harder to see the right side, the burns that have dominated his life. Matthew is alone, it's probably easier for him to cope that way.

But Matthew was standing there and I should have helped. I still feel weak, ashamed that I didn't do anything. It's so easy to think you'll react in a certain way. You think ahead and see yourself doing the right thing. The only true test is when it happens and you have to move, you have to stretch out a hand and help. That's not easy. Every year someone gets dragged out to sea or falls through some ice on a lake. Every time, whoever happens to be there has to face the test, they have to act. Even if it's hopeless, most people still dive into the sea or go out on to the ice. They might die trying. You don't hear about the ones who just stand and watch, who can't move because they're scared and can't make up their minds what to do. They have to live with it for the rest of their lives. Should I have helped? Would it have made any difference?

Those aren't easy questions to deal with.

Matthew got away. Maybe I would have gone in if Luke had started beating him. Maybe then I would have helped. Or I might have stood there in the bushes, watching it all happen in front of me, sweating, my heart racing, feeling the shame wash over me. I'll never know.

I come out of the woods and cross a small patch of grass to reach Sarah's street. It's the same as most of the street in my town, semi-detached houses, clean front porches with glass doors, a drive running up the side, small square gardens at front and back. I don't know why these houses have the front porch. No one ever uses them. I walk up the drive and knock on her back door.

'Hello, Robbie.'

It's her sister Kate. Sarah's parents both work until seven or eight in the evening. I don't see them very often. Kate's leaning on the door frame, studying me.

'You all right?'

'Yeah, I'm fine.'

'You look a bit out of it. You feeling unwell?'

'Nah. Sarah in?'

'She's upstairs.'

I walk through the kitchen and into the hall. Sarah's standing at the foot of the stairs smiling at me.

'Hey, thought you weren't coming.'

She comes up to me and kisses my cheek. I can smell the perfume on her neck. She's in a white T-shirt and faded jeans.

'Sorry. I got held up.'

'Something better to do?'

'No. I'll tell you upstairs.'

'D'you want a coffee?'

'Thanks.'

'Go on up.'

Her room overlooks the garden. I can see the houses stretching off, then the trees on the hill beyond them. I feel nervous. Her room's very tidy, ordered. The bed's been made. I always feel nervous in a girl's room, scared I'm going to break something, say something dumb. I haven't been out with many girls. Sarah comes back in, puts her lips to mine and kisses me.

'Kate says you look sick.' She's giggling.

'Kate talks too much. There's nothing wrong with me.'

I'm not sure whether to tell her about it. It's very quiet in the house. I don't want anything from the outside world to come into this room. But she can see I'm tense.

'Come on. What is it?'

'I saw Luke in the woods.'

'That idiot. He didn't say anything about us, did he?'

'Why should he?'

'No reason.'

14

She picks up her coffee and takes a sip. Luke used to be crazy about Sarah, but so was just about every guy in the school. Ryan nearly passed out when I told him we were together.

'He was after Matthew.'

'Who was?'

'Luke was. He was chasing after Matthew with some of his moronic buddies. I could have done something.'

'What do you mean?' She looks surprised, as though it's incredible to her that I'd want to get involved.

'I could have stopped it, helped him out. Nothing happened though. Matthew ran off.'

'Is this why you're late?' She's staring at me over the rim of her coffee cup.

'Yeah.'

'I thought you wanted to see me this afternoon.'

'I do.'

'Doesn't sound like it.' She's speaking very quietly, trying to make me feel guilty.

'Hey. It was bad. Luke was angry.'

'What's it got to do with you anyway? Is Matthew a friend of yours?'

'I don't really know him, no.'

'Matthew's weird. Who knows what he's been doing to wind Luke up? He gives me the creeps.'

'How?'

'He just does.'

For a second I'm worried that Sarah might

have a problem with Matthew just because of his scar and that would make her no better than Luke. There have been a couple of times in the last two weeks when I've realized that there are a lot of things about her that are a mystery to me. Sometimes it's hard to get a firm opinion from her, she just smiles and changes the subject or blocks the question. I decide to push for an answer.

'Because of his face you mean? Is that why you think he's weird?'

'No, of course not. That's not his fault.'

'Too right it's not. You can't say he's strange just because of the way he looks.'

'I know. But he doesn't even try to fit in with any of us, does he? I mean, he never makes the effort to talk or be sociable, be friendly or anything.'

'I should have done something.'

'Robbie, it doesn't matter. Let them run around the woods like children. We've got better things to do.'

She puts her cup down and kisses me again. I can't work out what she really thinks. But she's right. It doesn't matter. It's over. Now it's just us here in her room.

'Yeah, sorry. It's in the past now. I can't change what happened.'

It's so easy to be here with her, to lie back on the bed and kiss, holding her. I should have more faith in her. We need some time to talk and get to know

16

each other better, that's all. It still excites me just being with her. I try and put the woods out of my mind, to forget it all. I over-reacted. But I keep seeing Matthew working his way up the bank, covered in dirt, the way he looked at me before he dived into the bushes.

Chapter 2

I wake up in my own room. It's full of light. I didn't shut the curtains when I came in last night. My mother's knocking on the door.

'Yeah.'

If I don't see her in the evening she usually comes up to my room before leaving for work. I guess she's checking I haven't been out all night.

'Hi there. I brought you some tea.'

'Thanks. You look smart.'

She's in a dress and a jacket. Her normal work clothes are less formal.

'I'm meeting some parents. Have to at least make a token effort to impress them. We're asking for money again.'

She sits down by my desk.

'Were you out with Sarah again last night?'

'Yeah.'

'Lost track of time, did you?'

'I was back at half-ten, Mum.'

'You're seeing her a lot.'

'What's the money for?'

'A swift change of topic, Robbie, well done. We need a piano for one of the music groups. What are you up to today?'

I sit up in bed and stretch. It's good to have all the freedom of the summer ahead of me, to be able to choose exactly what I want to do.

'I might meet up with Ryan.'

'He rang last night. Your father rang as well. Sends his love.'

Her voice doesn't change when she mentions my father. She could be talking about anyone, not the man she was married to for all those years.

'I'll give him a ring tonight.'

'OK. I was just saying hello. Don't seem to see much of you these days.'

'I'll be home by the time you get back. Thanks for the tea.'

'See you later.'

I pull on some clothes, a Mambo long-sleeve I got in London last time I was down there, some black jeans and trainers, then go down to the kitchen and shake some cereal into a bowl. It's too early to call Ryan, he sleeps late, so I decide to wander down to the high street then double back to his house in an hour or two. It's already hot outside; the light's bright enough to hurt my eyes for a few minutes before they adjust. I walk down my street and take a turn and I'm on the high street. This is the quiet end, a few small shops, a car show-room. The morning shoppers are drifting out of their houses. As I walk down towards the centre the pavements start to fill up, the town gets noisier. I reach the main music store and stroll in, checking some of the CDs in a sale they've got on. A rock track I don't recognize is blasting out around the room. This shop has a book section as well, along the back wall. I'm circling around it when I see him, standing close to one of the shelves, his face pushed up to the pages of a book. It's Matthew.

I should have known that there was more to come after the events in the wood. In a small town like this it wasn't going to disappear, I was bound to see him or Luke eventually and be reminded of the way I behaved, my hesitation. But I'm surprised nonetheless. Life's rarely as clear-cut as you would like it to be. I stare at him over one of the CD racks, thinking how it's all come around for me to deal with again. I wonder if I could shuffle out without him seeing me but I know I'm going to have to face him. I don't want the whole thing hanging over me, feeling involved somehow, it's stupid. I'll apologize. I'll do that and then my guilt will be gone and I can get on with enjoying the summer. I walk past the CD rack and come up behind him.

'Matthew.'

He doesn't turn around.

'I'm reading.'

'I want a word.'

He's looking well dressed compared to

yesterday but his clothes are still scruffy. They look as though they were worn in a few years ago, blue jeans so faded they're almost white, a heavy shirt that's too big for him, scuffed black leather shoes.

'What about?'

'About yesterday. I wanted to say I was sorry.'

'For what?'

His voice is thin and high compared to mine, making him sound much younger than sixteen.

'Come on, Matthew. Will you hear me out?'

'All right.'

He puts the book back on the shelf and starts walking for the door, still not looking at me. I follow after him. When we get out on to the street it's busy with shoppers. There's a pedestrian square further along the high street; I nod my head in that direction and we start walking side by side.

'What was Luke after you for?'

It's strange talking with him. There have been all those years at school when we were in the same class and we never said a word, almost as though he couldn't speak or was a different species or something. Now it strikes me that I've never really heard his voice before. It's hard to try to understand someone when there's no talk, it's dehumanizing, you don't think of them as really being there.

'That's my business.'

'You must have done something pretty bad for him to come after you like that.'

'I don't think so. It's just something he doesn't understand, that's all. He'll never understand it.'

We've reached the square and there's a bench free on one side. We sit down at either end of it, keeping our distance.

'I felt bad about it. When you were coming out of that ditch, I thought maybe I should have done something. I'm not the type of person who just walks on by, you know.'

'You were yesterday.'

It hurts to hear him say that. He won't look at me. He stares straight ahead, into the mass of strolling pedestrians.

'I know, and I've been feeling terrible about it. I just wasn't sure if I . . . what I could have done. I didn't understand the situation.'

'It was fairly clear, I thought. There wasn't much doubt in my mind. They wanted to catch me and hurt me.'

'Then why did you mess around with Luke?'

Now he turns his head and speaks boldly.

'I'm not scared of Luke Fisher.'

'Oh, sure.'

'I'm not.'

I've never been this close to him. It's hard not to stare at the burn, it pulls your eyes to it, its dark colour tempting you to look. I concentrate on his eyes, trying to focus on them so he knows I'm not looking at the scars. And I see a strength in his eyes. He means what he says.

23

'I'm not scared of him. And what's it to you anyway? Why are you hassling me like this?'

This isn't going how I wanted it to. I didn't expect Matthew to take me on. I thought he was passive, that I'd humbly deliver my apology and that would be it. He would nod and say 'forget it' and I'd put it behind me. But he's pressurizing me. I'm almost angry with him for keeping me here but I know I shouldn't be.

'I believe you, Matthew, that you're not scared of him. I just wanted . . .'

'I don't care if you do or if you don't. You didn't help anyway.'

'I'm telling you now . . .'

'I don't need your help. You don't have to come to me and clear your conscience. Frankly, I wasn't expecting anything more than you did, Robbie, I'm surprised you even stopped. But it doesn't matter. I can look after myself.'

Two minutes of talk with him have changed my view of him completely. I thought I was in control of the situation but it's Matthew who's speaking the truth, who's making the stand.

'Matthew, you wouldn't last a minute with Luke.'

'I'll fight him if I have to. I'm not sure if it's worth it yet. That's why I ran away.'

'What do you mean?'

'I've said enough. You don't really care, Robbie. You're all happy with Sarah, you don't need my grief.'

24

He knows about Sarah. He's always there watching, so far in the background that you forget him, forget he knows something about you.

'The fact I'm here now shows that it means something to me.'

'Perhaps, but have you figured out what it is? It's best if you stay out of it. You've never wanted to be a friend of mine before.'

'This is different.'

'Oh, so suddenly you care? Suddenly you're interested in me? I don't think so. You just feel bad. You don't know anything about me.'

'You're some kind of psychologist, a mind-reader, are you?'

'I have to be suspicious of people, Robbie. I can't just coast like you, take it easy all the time. You see them?'

He points at the shoppers, the people outside a café, milling around the square, all of them enjoying the sun.

'Yeah. I have eyes.

'They look at you and they look at me in different ways, you understand? I've grown up with their looks. You don't notice them, the glances, the odd stare, but I pick it up. I have to live with it. All the time. Every shop, every street, I get that. And I know you're part of that too. This is the first time we've ever talked. Like I said, you're only here because you feel bad, and even then, it was an accident you saw me today, wasn't it?'

He can read my face. I look down at my feet, feeling ashamed under his stare.

'Yeah. I wasn't expecting to see you so soon.'

'Well, there you go. At least you're honest. It was an accident yesterday too. Stay out of it, Robbie.'

He stands up and starts walking away. I look after him in the crowd but my vision has changed now. I notice the stares, the heads turning, only a flicker across a face but I can see it, Matthew can probably feel it as he walks past. How can you live with something like that? It must have been there with him for as long as he can remember. But he wasn't bitter when we talked. He spoke the truth. I feel crushed by what he said, the quiet, persuasive tone of his voice telling me what I am. I knew this was going to come back on me, that it wasn't over yesterday, but I didn't guess it was going to be this hard. Our talk hasn't made me feel any better. If anything, it's driven home all my doubts about myself. Knowing a little more about him makes me feel worse. He's no longer just a scrawny kid hanging around at the back of the class, someone who doesn't fit in, someone to ignore. Talking with him I know him a little as a person now. He's a lot stronger than I imagined.

Ryan's still lying in bed when I push into his room. I have to push the door because there's trash all over the floor – clothes, magazines, boxes of junk.

The curtains are still shut and the room's quite dark.

'You should clean this place up.'

'Have a seat and stop lecturing me. Who let you in? My mum around then?'

'Yeah, she's downstairs.'

It's hard to find a place to stand in all the mess. I step towards the window.

'What time is it?'

I open the curtains and turn round to look at him. He's rubbing his eyes in the sunlight.

'It's about eleven, Ryan.'

'A dawn raid.'

'Hardly.'

I manage to shift a box from a chair and sit down. When I look over to him he's yawning, but I can tell he's waking up properly now. His voice is confident, the cheeky tone that I know so well.

'I tried calling you last night.'

'Yeah, I know.'

'You were ensconced with Sarah, no doubt. How's it going with the love goddess?'

'Good.'

Ryan crawls out of the bed and pulls on some trousers, checks himself in a mirror. He's tall, with long, curly red hair.

'Ah, what a body I have, what a face! Only kidding. You been up to anything else then, Robbie?'

Ryan's probably the closest friend I have. We can talk about anything.

'I've had a strange experience.'

'Indeed. Abducted by aliens?'

'No. I've been guilt-tripped by Matthew.'

He looks puzzled. 'Who's Matthew?'

'From our school, you know.'

'You mean the guy with the scar?'

'Yeah, him.'

He's working his way through the debris in his room, looking for some trainers.

'What happened?'

'I saw him out in the woods having a run-in with Luke. I could have done something but I froze.'

'A wise move, Robbie. I wondered what Luke was doing up in town.'

'What do you mean?'

'He's moved down to London.'

'Has he?'

Ryan hears all the news first. He loves to chat, exchange gossip with all the other kids at our school. He's much more sociable than I am.

'Yeah, only a few weeks ago. I saw him last night though and we had a chat. He was out of it, I think, drunk or something. Told me he'd come up to town to sort out some family business. I didn't push the interrogation past that. So what happened with you anyway?'

'I saw Matthew this morning, tried to sort it out, but I left feeling like I'd messed it up even more.'

Ryan doesn't look that impressed by my agonizing.

'You're not going to get any sense out of him. Why waste your time? He's crazy, isn't he?'

'No, he didn't come over like that to me.'

'You always were a soft touch, man. You worry too much about other people. Anyone like Matthew is probably adept at making everyone else feel bad, playing the sympathy angle. He's skilled at it, I reckon. You can't change anything with a guy like that. It's "Sob, sob, isn't my life awful?" all the time.'

Why does everyone think so badly of Matthew? I have to recall the way I thought about him before I saw him in the woods to understand Ryan's attitude. Now that I've spoken with Matthew everything's changed. He's no longer a shadow, someone to be ignored, criticized for no reason other than the fact he's an outsider.

'He wasn't like that with me. He was strong. I have to respect him. It was me who was in the wrong.'

'Forget it, Rob. These things work themselves out, don't worry. You want a drink?'

'If you're making one.'

He's always so relaxed. Ryan doesn't want any hassles in his life. I can tell he thinks I'm stupid for worrying.

'I'll see if I can get my mum to do the honours. I've been riding high on the sweeteners since the exams ended.'

'She hasn't seen your results yet.'

29

'That could be interesting, I agree. What do you want to do about college, have you made your mind up?'

My mind flicks round to thoughts of the autumn. 'I was keen on the London idea but, you know . . .'

'Sarah came along and whisked you off your feet.'

'You could say that. I'm not sure what she's planning on doing but I doubt if she wants to go down to London.'

Sarah's happy in our town. She likes having a large circle of friends and everyone likes her here. Also, there are all the accommodation problems of living in London. She's very close to her parents and I know she likes living at home.

'So you're that serious about her, Robbie? You'd stay here just to be with her? Are you sure it's going to last?'

'Who can say?'

'I mean, she's not renowned for longevity, is she? She moves around a bit.'

'Watch it, Ryan. We're into each other.'

Sometimes he pushes the cheek a little too far. He gets into trouble now and again with people who have less of a sense of humour than I do.

'How far have you gone with her?'

'I said watch it. Keep your nose out.'

'Ah, I see. Haven't done anything then.'

'It's developing slowly.'

I'm not in the mood to discuss my love life with him but he's grinning, enjoying himself.

'Well, if you make it with her she must be serious. She hasn't gone with anyone else as far as I know.'

'Ryan. Cut it out, all right? I've got a few other things on my mind right now.'

It's typical that he knows this information about Sarah. If anything happens in this town Ryan seems to find out. He talks so openly about everything. Ryan's easygoing, he doesn't take life too seriously. He started revising for the exams the night before they started but he'll probably do all right, he's intelligent. I think we get on because we're quite different. I tend to worry about things more than he does, dwell on them, turn them over in my mind. He just gets on with it, speaks before thinking. He's so casual, the way he asked if Sarah and I were sleeping together yet. I don't want to pressure Sarah but in a way it's been the other way round. Her father's flat was a clue, she's easing me towards the idea. There are days when I can't think of anything else but at the same time I'm in no rush, it'll happen. This business with Matthew has interrupted all that.

'What do you think I should do?'

'Start carrying protection with you day and night.'

'I mean about Matthew.'

'Do nothing. Luke'll probably get so wrecked he'll forget about it. Anyway, I don't see what it's got to do with you.'

Again the discussion comes round to this point. I think about it for a moment and it does make sense. Even Matthew told me to stay out of it.

'You're right. It's not my business.'

'Yeah. I don't know why you're interested in anything but Sarah, she's gorgeous. And London maybe.'

Ryan is desperate to get down to London. He's a party animal, loves the big city.

'I'm still thinking about London, Ryan, don't worry. The great escape. Civilization.'

'Truth. You're not going to find a lot of action here next year. Everyone's moving out. Maybe you should try and talk Sarah into it. Let's have that drink.'

'Yeah, then I should get back into town. I was going to check on a few things. I didn't get a chance earlier.'

'I'll come in with you.'

It feels good walking around the town with Ryan, back to normality after the encounter with Matthew. We check a few of the shops, go for some drinks in a café and meet up with some of our year. Everyone's in good spirits, relaxed after the exams. I'm working my way through a coffee, arguing with Ryan about a movie we've both seen, when Sarah comes into the room. She's got some relatives visiting her house today, I thought she was going to be busy. I stand up from the table and walk over.

'Hi. Didn't expect to see you.'

'I had to come into town to get some stuff for dinner, thought I'd make a quick search and see if I could find you.'

'I'm glad you did. I'm with Ryan.'

When Sarah comes into a room there's a perceptible change of atmosphere. Men stare at her, women notice her. It's not just lust or envy. Sarah is an event. She's so striking to look at that people pause in whatever they're doing, they check her out. It gives me an odd feeling being with a girl who's so attractive. In some ways it makes me feel good, gives me a lift, but it also worries me. I'm not the jealous, possessive type but it would be justifiable with Sarah. Guys are on the make with her all the time. Not that she will act on it. It's the propositions themselves that make me nervous. I realize that she is *desired*. She doesn't play up to it but she does know the power she has. She's aware of it.

'Hi, Ryan.'

'All right, Sarah.'

She sits down and takes a sip from my coffee cup. Then she leans back in her chair and smiles at me, looking a little proud of herself.

'I've got some news for you.'

'Yeah.'

I'm staring at her. It takes me a minute or two for it to sink in that it's me she's dating. I know that looks aren't everything. In fact, I know they don't mean much at all when it comes to having a serious

33

relationship. They're only surface. What matters is what's inside. But Sarah's so good-looking I'm slightly in awe of her. I can't help it.

'Robbie, are you listening to me?'

'Yeah. What's the news then?'

'It's about the Luke and Matthew incident that shook you up so much. Well, it's all about Luke's sister actually.'

'Cassie?'

'Yeah. Matthew has declared his undying love for Cassie.'

Ryan breaks out laughing.

'You're kidding.'

'No. I saw Ruth, from my class, you know, this morning and she told me all about it. Apparently Matthew was sending Cassie all these love letters and Luke found one. I don't know how Cassie kept it quiet. I'd have thought she'd have passed them all around the school. They must be a scream. Can you imagine Matthew and his love poetry?'

Ryan's rocking with laughter. Sarah's talking to him now, they're joking with one another about it, trying to guess what Matthew might have written. I feel left out of the conversation. Just a few minutes' talk with Matthew and I have such a different opinion of him than they do. Sarah turns back to me.

'Luke's not exactly pleased about it, Robbie. That's why he was chasing after him.'

'He was always very protective of his sister.'

34

'He doesn't want her teaming up with Matthew, that's for sure. Luke's a proper fascist, he's always hated anyone who's a bit weird, he's not going to be tolerant about his sister seeing a cripple.'

'Matthew's not crippled.'

'You know what I mean.'

'I wonder if he'll be heading back to London soon.'

'No, he's not going back until it's been settled. And from what Ruth's saying it could be very nasty. Matthew's days are numbered.'

'Sarah. You're talking about a kid from our school. I don't think it's funny that Luke's after him.'

'I'm only joking. I think it's hilarious that Matthew's fallen in love with Cassie. She won't go near any of the blokes at school. Not surprising, they're all terrified of Luke . . .'

I'm thinking back to what Matthew was saying this morning, trying to make sense of his words. He's really not scared of Luke. Sarah's proved that by what she's just said. But I think he was saying something else as well. I can't remember it clearly. About whether it was 'worth it' or not. I wish I'd paid more attention to him.

'Besides, Luke won't kill him, he's not that stupid.'

Ryan cuts in. 'Luke's been getting a bit out of control lately with the drinking though. Half the time he doesn't know where he is. Maybe Matthew should keep a low profile for a while. What a mess. I haven't seen Cassie around for a while, have you? Luke must have locked her up at home.'

Cassie's in our year at school. I don't know her very well, she's quite private, nothing like Luke. She's small and pretty and seems to be off in a dream world most of the time. Sarah doesn't get on with her that well. She finds Cassie a bit serious.

'I don't fancy Matthew's chances, with Cassie or Luke. But it's strange, isn't it? I wonder what Matthew was thinking.'

'Sarah, why shouldn't Matthew be into her?'

'Come on, Robbie. He's being a little optimistic, don't you think?'

There's a sneer on her face. I try to defend Matthew.

'It's not all about the way he looks.'

'I know. That wasn't what I was saying.'

She's leaning in close to me now. She puts her hand out and touches mine.

'I didn't mean that. But he's never even spoken with her.'

'How do we know that?'

Ryan drops some coins on the table.

'Let's move on from here. I have to get back.'

Sarah glances at her watch.

'Yeah, I should head for home. They're expecting me to do some of the cooking.'

Ryan stand up and makes for the door.

'I'll be outside, Robbie.'

'Yeah.'

Sarah kisses me.

'You're not mad with me about anything, are you?'

'No. What makes you think that?'

'You seem a bit cold to me.'

'It's just all this hassle for Matthew. I'm thinking it over, that's all. I saw him this morning but he didn't mention Cassie.'

'He probably wants to be left alone.'

'Yeah.'

'Can we meet up tomorrow? My dad's place is empty.'

'Sounds good. I'll give you a ring tonight.'

'You can give me a kiss now, can't you?'

'Of course.'

I hold her tight and kiss her, then we walk out of the café, arm in arm.

When I get home I make a sandwich and flop into an armchair. My mother isn't back yet. I'm feeling tense. Sarah didn't exactly come out and say it but I could tell what she was thinking about Matthew and Cassie getting together. She takes so much for granted, she's got nothing to worry about with her looks, quite the opposite. She's popular and she'll do well in the exams. Twenty-four hours ago Matthew was non-existent in my thinking but now I can't get him out of my mind. I keep telling myself that they're right, everyone tells me it's got nothing to do with me, but I feel somehow involved. I decide to mention it to my mother. I know she'll understand how I'm thinking. There have been a few times in the last year or two when I've gone to her with a problem and she's given me advice, helped me think it through. Everyone comes to her with their problems. I guess that comes with the job she does as well. She has to listen to people, help them. She tries to be considerate, never pushes her own opinion on you, just hints at it.

I hear the kitchen door open and go in to meet her. She looks tired.

'What a day. I can't wear clothes like this in the heat.'

'How did the fund-raising go?'

She heads over to the fridge and pours herself an orange juice.

'Want one?'

I shake my head. She sits down at the table.

'I think we'll get the money. It's sad the school has to do so much begging but the grant keeps being cut. What have you been doing?'

'I went into town, met up with Ryan.'

'Did you call your father?'

It's unusual for her to remind me of things like this about him. There must be something going on.

'No. I was going to do it this evening.'

'Normally I'd agree. I can't face the phone bills

we're getting. But this is important, Robbie.'

'What is it?'

'I've got a few things to tell you. Let's go and sit down next door.'

We go through to the living-room and I sink back into the armchair. I look up at her.

'I have to talk with you about something too, Mum. It's been bugging me all day.'

'I should tell you about your father's call first. Robbie, he wants to meet up with you.'

'I was thinking of going over there in a week or two. There's a concert on I wouldn't mind seeing. Thought I might see if he'd let me and Sarah stay at the flat.'

He hasn't met Sarah yet, I've been avoiding the moment. But she keeps asking me if we can go and stay in London at his flat. She's heard of the area he lives in and seems impressed. I think she imagines the flat's going to be some kind of mansion.

'He's moving. He's moving out of the country. Soon.'

'Out of the country? Where to?'

'His company's expanding. For a change he seems to be doing well. He's going over to live in Singapore.'

'That's the other side of the planet.'

'I know.'

London's only thirty miles away and I rarely see him. What's it going to be like with him living out there?

'He might ask you to go over there some time, Robbie. It's not as though it's for ever. He wants to see you in London in the next day or two. He wasn't supposed to be leaving for another two months but he's had to change his plans.'

'Well, this is news. I don't know what to say.'

I stare over at her and I can see there's more to come.

'What else?'

'This isn't the best timing but I should tell you now. I've met someone.'

'You've done what?'

'I've met a man. I've known him for a few months but I thought we were just friends. That's changed. So, he's coming round for dinner and I thought you could meet him.'

'Round here? When's this happening?'

'Tonight.'

She's staring intently at me. I don't want to make her unhappy but I'm confused. What does she expect me to say? I have to put things in perspective. My father and I have some problems but that doesn't mean I want him to live six thousand miles away.

'I can't believe you're asking some guy around at the same time as telling me Dad's vanishing.'

'I know it's sudden but I wanted you to meet him as soon as possible. I thought you should know. As for your father – well, there's nothing I can say that will change what he does. It didn't make any difference when we were married, Robbie. It's really nothing to do with me. I'm sorry that you won't be able to see him as much as you'd like to.'

'What's your new boyfriend called?'

'Jeff.'

I hadn't guessed she'd been seeing anyone lately. I feel as though I've been kept in the dark about her and my father.

'You could have told me before. It's not much warning for dinner, is it?'

'You've been out with Sarah a lot. Before that I didn't want to distract you from your exams. I should have told you this morning but I thought you should speak to your father first, I thought that would be more important for you.'

'No offence to Jeff but it is, yeah. What time's he coming?'

'Eight.'

And no escape to Sarah tonight, she's busy entertaining her relatives. I could call Ryan.

'You will meet him, won't you?'

'I don't see why you're so bothered.'

'I'd like you to meet him. I think you'd get on. It's important to me.'

'I should call Dad, find out when he wants me to go down there. But I'll be here for dinner.'

'What did you want to talk about? I haven't given you much of a chance to speak, sorry.'

'It can wait.'

I leave the room and go through to the kitchen. The phone's mounted on the wall. I feel worse than I did when I got in. I can't believe I've been worrying so much about Matthew and his problems when my own life is suddenly changing with every breath. I put it to the back of my mind and dial my father's number.

'Hi, Dad.'

'Robbie. She told you then?'

'Yes. Just a minute ago.'

'What do you think? Some life in your father yet! You are coming over to see me, aren't you? Christmas? How d'you fancy Christmas by a pool?'

'It's too alien for me to think about. I've never been out of England before. Sounds different, Dad.'

It's almost five o'clock. My father's probably half-way through his first bottle of wine by now. He starts drinking at lunchtime and finishes with a nightcap just before midnight. But it doesn't seem to damage his work – his world runs around alcohol. His clients are always entertained in restaurants or function halls, champagne spilling everywhere, white wine with the first course, red for the second, port and brandy later. A lot of his business comes from these dinners or similar events, contacting, chatting over a beer after a meeting, picking up the news. He told me once that you have to be able to take your drink if you want to be in commerce, that it's all part of the business game.

'It's a bit of a rush, Robbie. Can you come over tomorrow?'

'I had a few things to do but I can get out of them. I'll get the eleven o'clock train.'

'Great. Get a cab from the station and I'll pay him when you get here.'

'I'll get the tube. It's not a problem.'

'As you wish. You sound like your mother. I'll see you tomorrow then.'

He's always brief with me on the phone. I remember him being on the phone for hours when we lived in London, talking with his business friends, but with me he's impatient to get off.

'Tomorrow, Dad.'

I put the phone down and go up to my room. I've got a lot of things to mull over before Jeff arrives for dinner.

Chapter 3

The morning rush has died down by the time I get to the station. My town is full of commuters. Between seven and half-past eight in the morning they line up on the London platform, reading papers, checking their ties. Some of them are so familiar with the routine they wait in exactly the right spot for the carriage door when the train pulls to a stop. They've had the same seat, the same conversations and company job for years. That kind of career is changing, the same job for life, but there are still lots of people in my town who are part of it, the office brigade. I buy a ticket and wander out on to the platform. I could have taken the bus, it's a bit quicker, but I like riding the train. It gives me more of a chance to think as I drift past the fields and into the suburbs of London. I'm catching a Sprinter. I know the times so I only wait two or three minutes before it rolls up. A few others climb aboard with me – two girls I vaguely know from school (I nod a hello), a middle-aged couple and two or three guys in suits.

The train pulls out and we're soon in the country-side, the sun colouring everything with summer light.

It feels good heading into London. I haven't been down there for over a month. But I'd prefer it if it wasn't a farewell visit to my father. It could be awkward seeing him. I got the impression on the phone that he was only asking me down because he felt he should make the effort, try a bit of the 'father bonding with son' approach. I'll probably catch the train back tonight. If I hang around too long the conversation will start running thin. When I meet up with him in town we usually just have lunch, then I go out roaming around the city. Most evenings he's out with a client or having a dinner party so I just catch up with him to say good-night. We operate on this system, short bursts of each other. That way we never have to go further than the light chit-chat, the 'how's school going' stuff. But this is different. I've been sum-moned. There's no way to avoid having some real talk.

It isn't going to change my life much, him leav-ing. He's never been a big part of my life anyway. However, he's still a presence, I've known he was there. After my parents broke up I had to get used to the fact that situations change, I couldn't be as sure about everything as I had been before. I grew up a lot. It made me realize that my parents were real people, human, with all the desires and faults

46

that go with it. Ryan's folks are still together. I can tell he still views them as some kind of stable guardians, never veering from the path that he considers 'normal'. You don't have to face it unless they break up. It'll probably happen to Ryan later in life, with the first ugly break-up or emotional tangle of a love affair. Some people can go through their whole lives without having to deal with it. You could stay in my town, work there, fall in love with someone and pass a lifetime in bliss. But I think most people will see those childhood foundations of security and naivety shattered at some point. It took me a long time to stop hating my father, because I saw my family as a unit for my development which he had abandoned. I wasn't as crucial to him as I had thought. He was prepared to wreck it all. Eventually I realized he's just a person and of course we all make mistakes and change our minds, change our lives.

My mother's found Jeff. She's changing her life again. There have been a couple of guys around over the years but no one I thought would last. This guy's in with a chance. I was expecting a nightmare dinner experience, a guy in a suit, loaded down with flowers and chocolates, a big handshake for the kid he's supposed to get on with. It's always different from how you imagine it's going to be. Jeff's a musician. I thought he'd be a teacher or a librarian, quiet and sensitive, bookish. He was the opposite, he dominated the conversation with

47

anecdotes about his travels around the world, full of energy. My mother stared at him as though he was giving off some kind of magical glow. He's a classical musician, not a rock star but a fairly wild guy all the same. I'd put him in his early forties. We got on all right. He didn't try too hard to come over as my future friend. I went up to my room after the meal and I could hear them talking until I turned out the lights and shut my eyes. I think she's crazy about him. She obviously goes for the strong characters, can't help herself. Jeff reminded me a little of my father.

Sarah was angry that she wasn't going to see me today. I rang her before dinner. If I'm not too late back I might give her a call tonight but she wanted to spend the afternoon round at the flat. I think she's used to being worshipped, obeyed. It was satisfying in a strange way, telling her I had to cancel. I'm not going to be a sycophant. Having said that, it was easier to say it on the phone. If she'd been next to me I might have thought twice about it. It's crazy that someone's appearance can be so powerful, have an effect on me the way she does.

The train is already rumbling through the decaying industry of the South London river-banks: dead warehouses, cobbled streets, dirty little shops, all of them in the tableau from the elevated railway line. I can see the slated roofs and council blocks of London's millions, the offices and pomp of the centre up ahead of me. As we crawl into

Waterloo I decide to take my father up on his offer and get the cab after all. I want to see the city flash by rather than be stuck in a tunnel deep in the earth. Anyway, he's paying and he wants to pay. I'd never take a cab with my mother or on my own but it's one of his ways of greeting his son. He believes in money.

There's a line of taxis outside the station. I give the address and hop in the back. It takes about twenty minutes through the traffic, rushing through the chaos of Trafalgar Square, up the long avenue and past the Queen's pad then out through Knightsbridge. London looks alive. Cocooned in the back of a cab you can watch all the noise and mania of the city flash by. The people are so much more cosmopolitan, more varied in race, age and status, than the lazy shoppers and tired stock-brokers of my town. Here all life's dramas are played out, so many faces in the crowd, one second a pack of youths, then a man covered in news-papers, sleeping in a doorway as the city bustles around him, now two old men in formal suits, talk-ing business as they pace past. I love London. Not only is it the place where you come to stand out, to succeed and make yourself, but you can also lose yourself in the throng. You never see the same stranger twice, the faces are always changing. No matter how many times you come here you can never know all the places, all the bars, restaurants, shops and clubs. The city is too vast to become familiar. I see a man loping past a shop window, in a ripped leather jacket and beach-bum shorts, his hair bleached white and silver rings in his nose and eyebrow. He doesn't attract any stares, any surprise. He's normal here. Everyone is normal.

And of course I think about Matthew. He could submerge himself here if he wanted, lose himself in the crowd. Then I realize the truth, that for Matthew it will never be like that. Even here he'd still have problems. I was thinking of people who *choose* to look different, people who perhaps do that because they react against the anonymity of the city, a society where no one is noticed. But Matthew would be. He'll always have to meet with other people, work with someone, shop for food, the simple things that mean nothing to most people. But Matthew will get the same looks he does in our town, feel the mark on his face in every simple environment. I'd forgotten about him, with my father and Jeff to deal with. I stop looking out at the city and stare at the floor of the cab. I'm still confused about Matthew. After the talk with him I feel as though I know something about him but I'm unsettled, it's not right in my head yet. I should go to see him. Ryan was right about Luke. Matthew has to get out of his way for a while. I'll see him, warn him that Luke's not giving up. I want to know about Cassie, if he'll tell me, I'm curious.

'Whereabouts d'you want?'

I look up and we're outside my father's flat, a tall London town house that's been broken up into apartments.

'This is it. Just here.'

He stops the cab and I climb out. There are some steps up to the front door of the house. Sasha, my dad's girlfriend, is sitting out in the sun on the top step, a glass of wine balanced in her hand.

'Hello, Robbie. Phillip's just popped out. He left you this.'

She takes a long sip from her glass and lifts a twenty-pound note into the air, waves it. I trail up the steps to take it from her. She doesn't let go for a second, teasing me, then she releases her grip.

'Thanks.'

I pay the cab driver and watch him drive off.

'You haven't brought a bag with your things.'

'I don't think I'm staying.'

'Oh, Phillip will be disappointed.'

I don't like hearing my father's first name. It sounds like he's a teenager. It also feels weird him calling Sasha his 'girlfriend'. It's all contrary to the formality that I came to expect between my parents, and when it went it took a long time to get used to the change. Some of it I still have problems with. She's wearing a white dress that leaves her arms and shoulders bare. She's tanned. They go away on holiday a lot.

'He'll be back in a minute, Robbie.'

'It's hot, isn't it?'

'Lovely. Would you like a glass of wine?'

'No thanks.'

I sit down next to her on the step. When I first met her she was only twenty-six, so she's still in her mid-thirties. She looks a lot younger than my mother. I think she works out, spends money on her looks. I remember my father telling me he'd joined a health club a while ago and I know it was under her influence. As he gets older he's probably scared of losing her to a younger man. Once you've broken off a relationship I guess you know how easily it could happen to you.

'Don't you drink wine?'

'Sometimes.'

'I love wine. I hope we can find some good wine when we're over there.'

She's like a cat, curled around her glass, leaning back against the cold stone of the house, trying to find some shade. She always sounds as though she's just woken up.

'I don't know what the Singaporeans think about drinking. I didn't think you'd be going anyway. What about your job?'

Sasha comes over as a bimbo but it's just an act. She's a solicitor and I wouldn't be surprised if she earns more than my father does. She works for a big firm in the City.

'It's a happy coincidence that my company has offices out there. I'll be working part-time.'

'Robbie, you made it.'

It's my father, standing at the foot of the steps. He's in a suit, as he always is. If I ever went mountain-climbing with him he'd still wear a suit. He's holding a plastic bag.

'Had to get some groceries. Sasha's cooking us lunch.'

'Great.'

He strides up the steps, leans over and kisses Sasha on the cheek.

'Let's go in. I want to hear what you've been up to. We've got a lot to discuss.'

My father's flat spreads out over two floors. The ground floor is a huge living-room with a kitchen at the back. There's a cast-iron spiral staircase that leads up to the bedrooms and a rear balcony that hangs over the garden. The room looks exactly the way I remember it, with the addition of a few boxes and packages near the windows. The bookshelves have been stripped.

'Done all your packing?'

'You know me, I travel light. I'm only taking a few suitcases. We've sent some boxes on but this is going into storage.'

'So what's happening with the flat? Are you selling it?'

'No, but before you visualize yourself partying here at the weekends I should tell you we're letting it. Someone's offered us an insane amount of money for it.'

53

'So you're only going for a year or something then? If you're hiring it out to someone.'

'We're doing it through an agency. I think it'll be a bit longer than a year. But you've only just arrived. Have a seat. We've got lots of time to talk.'

Sasha goes back to the kitchen and fills her glass from a bottle on the side.

'Robbie has to go back tonight.'

'Why's that?'

'I've got a lot going on at the moment.'

'But it's the summer. I remember you always being so bored in the summer.'

I don't want to mention Sarah. He might crack some jokes and anyway it's my personal life, he doesn't need to know about it.

'I have to see someone. You didn't give me much time to play with, did you? When are you going?'

'Three days. How's your mother?'

'She's well. Everything's fine.'

'The exams go all right?'

'Yeah, I think so.'

'Good on you, Robbie. So how about a drink to celebrate?'

'Maybe later. It's early and I haven't eaten anything.'

'Very responsible. I'll have a glass of whatever you're drinking, Sash.'

She fills a wine glass and leaves it on the side of the table for him.

'So why the move all of a sudden? I thought you were happy here in London.'

'We are but I'm opening a new office out there. Besides, this could be my last great adventure.'

'Phillip?'

Sasha gives him a mock stern look. She's laying bowls of food on to a heavy oak table they have in the kitchen. My father goes over and starts helping her.

'You only get the chance to try a few things in your life. I've fancied living in the East for a long time. And in a couple of years I won't be able to do so much travelling.'

'You sound like you've been given only a few years to live.'

'In a way that's correct, Robbie.'

'I don't understand.'

'Sasha and I have decided to have a child together.'

I stare up at him from the table. He looks proud, as though he wants me to leap up from my seat and hug him. Instead, I look over at Sasha.

'Are you having a baby?'

She breaks into laughter. 'Very tactful, Robbie. No, I am not "having a baby". But we're going to. I'll be able to stop working in two or three years and I think that will be a good time to do it.'

'So why announce it now?'

'Because that's one of the reasons why we're going abroad. It's our last freedom fling. An adventure, as your father said.'

She blushes. Obviously she'd forgotten that my father was supposed to have finished his 'adventures' with children when I was born.

My father cuts in. 'I thought I'd prepare you before we went anyway. When we get back you might have a sister or a brother. We'll come back to England to bring the child up, of course.'

They have no obstacles in their life together. They've got enough money to do what they want and Sasha's young enough to have a baby. I always assumed she didn't want children. But it's a second chance for him, an action replay of his life and this time he can shape it the way he wants. I feel empty, like an intruder in their house. I feel like saying, 'You messed up with me, why should this one be any different, what did I do wrong?' He's only thinking about a child as a symbol of their love (if they really do love one another) and of his virility. The child doesn't matter to him. I feel angry and powerless. I want to speak out, to protest.

'That would be great.'

I can only say what he wants to hear. The people in his life are just objects that he expects to behave in certain ways, but he's my father. He always has that insurance, that last bond which I'm too scared to break; it's a power over me. I've lost count of the times when I've thought of telling him I never want to see him again but I couldn't bring myself to do it. And now, that thing that I've worried about so much, he can do it without giving it a thought. He decides to leave the country, arranges a farewell chat, see you in a few years and by the way I'm going to start another family. The last one didn't work out too well. He does exactly what he wants.

'Let's have lunch.'

Sasha's made some Italian food, strips of chicken in a spicy tomato sauce, some pasta shells with fresh herbs and a green salad. I chomp my way through the meal, staring out of the window, joining in with the small talk. They quaff their way through another bottle of white wine. I stick with orange juice. When we've finished Sasha leaves the table and heads upstairs to sleep for a couple of hours. It emerges that they're going out to a function tonight. They wouldn't have been around even if I had decided to stay. I help him with the clearing up.

'I'll only be a phone call away, Robbie, and I'll write. If we get a large enough place I'll send you an air ticket over there.'

'I'm not sure what I'll be doing next year, Dad.'

'And on your eighteenth I'm going to buy you a car. There'll be a fat cheque in the post for you, don't worry.'

'I'll look forward to it.'

'Do you want to go into town, do a bit of shopping? I'm going to give you some money.'

'I should get back.'

'It hasn't been much of a leaving party, has it?'

For a second I think it might change. Maybe we'll talk like two friends and I can ask him all the things I want to. He's not looking at me. He's rinsing some glasses, stacking them in the drainer. He sounded genuine, as though he was introducing a bridge in the conversation so we could get round to some truth, discuss how I feel about him and what he's doing. But there have been moments like this before. Sometimes he stops his charge through life and reflects. He's always pushing, trying to find the next change, but once in a while he pauses. I give it a go anyway.

'The baby idea was unexpected.'

'I thought it might be. I should have left it until we knew for sure. I don't even know if we'll be able to.'

'Have you told Mum?'

'No. I don't think she'd be interested, do you?'

'I don't know what she'll say.'

'You have to try these things, Robbie. What I was saying earlier about Singapore being the adventure, well, it will be, but the idea of having another child, that's the real adventure.'

The pain is coming back. He goes on talking, not noticing the way I must be looking.

'Find out what's important to you and do it. Sometimes it's only a feeling at the back of your mind, you're not certain about it until the last moment, but you have to find out. Then you know what you have to do. And it all falls into place.'

I don't argue with him. Other times in the past we've rowed. There's no point. I have to take him as he is. And I agree with some of what he says anyway. What I find difficult is the flexibility he allows himself. His 'certainty' doesn't last for ever, it's just how he feels at the time.

'I won't see you again before you go then?'

'I'll call you. I'll be in touch.'

'All right. I should start thinking about the train.'

'I've got a taxi number, it's on the mantelpiece.'

I shuffle in and out of his life in taxi cabs. He never comes to the station to meet me or see me off. I'm just another visitor.

Before I leave he gives me a fifty-pound note and tells me to celebrate the exam results. He shakes my hand and I wish him a good time in the Orient, then I'm in the cab and on my way back to the station. I don't ever want to be like him. It's a hard thing not wanting to be like your father.

It's still light when I get back. I was only in London for four hours, a fleeting visit. My mother's reading in the living-room, surrounded by piles of school papers and files.

'How was the big smoke?'

'Fine.'

'Your father his usual cheery self?'

'Absolutely. He doesn't change. I liked Jeff. Are you going to be seeing a bit of him?'

She doesn't say anything for a moment, then she turns to me and speaks confidently. 'I think so, yes. I'm sorry it was all a bit rushed, with your father going away and everything.'

'Don't worry about it. I've been brooding about something else actually, been preoccupied by it.'

'What's that?'

She puts down the file she was holding and sits back in her chair.

'This kid from my school, called Matthew.'

'Matthew Bright?'

'I'm not sure. That might be his surname. Do you know him?'

'I know his mother. I've met her a few times. What's going on?'

'Something happened the other day and I keep thinking about it. I keep having other things to deal with, Sarah and Dad, you know, but I'm always coming around to this same kid.'

'Well, it must be important. If I've got a problem then I can get reminded of it by anything.'

'It's complicated. I think you'll be disappointed in me when I tell you.'

She laughs. 'No, you've never let me down before, Robbie.'

'I saw him being chased by someone, he was outnumbered and I didn't step in to help. Then I spoke with him later and he didn't want my help anyway. He turned it around on me so I feel even worse.'

She's looking more serious now, obviously concerned with what I've told her.

'Matthew's had a tough time. His disfigurement is something most people couldn't cope with. I've spoken with his mother about it but she's got her own problems too, Robbie. Don't feel bad about not helping him the first time. If you can do something now then do it. I get the feeling it's not over.'

'No, it's not. What did you mean about his mother?'

'I can't talk about that really. I can tell you that she relies on Matthew a lot though.'

'She does? I thought it would be the other way round.'

'No, she puts a lot of pressure on him. I don't think she could get by without him.'

'You know a lot about this.'

'Well, I run help sessions after school, remember. I've talked with her and Matthew.'

My mother worked for the Citizens' Advice Bureau and other groups in London, in her spare time. When she got the job at the school she started working after hours with parents and kids if they had problems to talk through. She doesn't mention it to me very often, as all the sessions are confidential.

'You can tell me about it. I mean, we already know a little about her at school.'

'I'll tell you because I know there's a lot of gossip about her, precisely those sort of rumours I think you're getting at. That's the biggest problem with a small town like this. There's so much talk flying around, most of it inaccurate. I'd rather you knew the truth. Anyway, it's hardly a secret. Matthew's mother is an alcoholic. He looks after her when it gets bad. That's why you don't see him about very much. He has to spend a lot of time with her, you see, Robbie.'

'I thought it was his face that made him nervous about that.'

'I'm sure it plays a part. Have you spoken much with Matthew before?'

'No. He's always kept himself to himself. I think he could have fitted in a lot better at school if he'd made the effort, you know, made a lot of friends. Once everyone knew about him, got on with him, then his face wouldn't matter.'

The tone of her voice changes now. She sounds almost frustrated. 'Maybe he doesn't want to play along with that.'

'I don't follow you.'

'Well, I see a lot of that with kids who have problems with their appearance. They can become one of the gang if they act up for the others, become the class comedian or try to impress in other ways. But maybe Matthew doesn't think he should have to be anything else but himself to deserve friendship.'

'I still don't get you.'

'I think he coped with his scarring by thinking it

wasn't there, that it was invisible and wouldn't affect him. Then when he realized that he was stigmatized by it he became angry and maybe a little bitter. It's driven him into himself a bit. But I think it'll all work out for Matthew in the end. He's very strong, Robbie.'

It's good to hear her confirm my own feelings but I'm puzzled that she's been able to learn so much about him.

'You know all about it. I don't understand.'

'When his mother was coming to see me he'd come with her. After a while he came on his own a few times. We talked.'

'You said he had to cope with the burns on his face. I thought it must have happened when he was a kid, when he was too young to remember.'

'He was ten or eleven, I'm not sure.'

She looks tired and distracted, as though the conversation is bringing back some feelings she'd forgotten, difficult feelings for her to deal with. She's so patient with me, didn't judge me for not helping him. The troubles I have talking with my father mean I've always relied on her for advice and support. She's had to deal with all my problems on her own, with no one to share the load.

'I'm going to see him. I'll see him in the morning.'

'You do that. His problems are so unfair, more so than you realize, it was all so unnecessary. So stupid.'

'What do you mean?'

'There are some things I can't tell you, Robbie. I've probably said too much already. Why don't you try and get to know him a bit better? I have to finish this work before I go to bed. Are you going over to Sarah's?'

'I'm going to call her but I think she said she was going out. Revenge for me going up to town.'

'I see. She's probably sitting at home waiting for you to call.'

I want to ask her some more questions. Every time I think I'm close to understanding Matthew something comes up and blurs the picture again. Just a few more minutes' talk. But the phone rings and she stares at me, waiting for me to go and answer it.

'That'll be her now, Robbie.'

I get up from my chair and pace through to the kitchen. It's Ryan.

'What you up to? You want to go out tonight?'

He sounds lively, whereas I'm suddenly aware of the fact that I'm exhausted.

'Hi, Ryan. No, I don't think I'm going to come out this evening. I've been in London and I'm really tired, I might crash out early.'

'Yeah, I was wondering what you were doing at home, thought you'd be out with Sarah. Your mother's been like an answer-machine lately.'

'I'll meet up with you tomorrow.'

'Are you coming along to Ruth's party?'

'I didn't know about it.'

'Sarah's helping to organize it, so I'm sure you'll get the invite.'

'It sounds good.'

'I'll see you there then.'

Sarah had mentioned some party to me but I thought it was a long way off. The time's been racing by. I call Sarah's number but there's no answer. So much for her waiting by the phone. I'd like to see her but at the same time I'm relieved she's not there. The day in town has fatigued me. I say good-night to my mother and head upstairs. After an hour flicking through a music magazine I'm feeling shattered so I kill the lights and drift off into sleep.

Chapter 4

I sleep late. It's past ten when I check the clock by my bed, rubbing bleary eyes and yawning. I get dressed and go down to the kitchen. My mother's already left the house. I make a drink and call Sarah.

'Where've you been, Robbie? I thought you'd call me last night.'

'I did. There was no answer.'

'I was out for an hour or two, round at Ruth's. You haven't forgotten she's having a party tonight, have you? It should be packed, we were ringing around checking who was coming.'

She was ringing all her friends but didn't manage to call me. But I don't want to get irritated with her, she sounds excited about the party.

'I'll be there.'

'Good. I want a chance to show you off.'

'It's the other way round, Sarah.'

'Flattery will get you everywhere. How was it with your dad?'

She sounds like she's skipping around her

house, she's so cheerful. She loves parties. I can imagine her and Ruth making the plans, predicting what will happen and with whom.

'A nightmare. I'll tell you later. When are we going to meet up?'

'I'll be at Ruth's most of the day. Drop in this afternoon.'

'Are we going to get any time alone?'

I want to speak with her, tell her everything that's been happening.

'We had all of yesterday to be alone. But we've got tomorrow if you want. I think the place is empty.'

'It's a date.'

'Look, I have to go. Ruth's expecting me.'

'I'll see you this afternoon. I missed you yesterday.'

'Me too. See you later.'

She's in full party mode, bubbling. She'll be busy all day and it gives me a chance to get in touch with Matthew. I want to talk with him and I have to warn him about Luke. I dig the phone book out of the cupboard and start checking the names. I'll call him and see if he wants to meet me. There are two Brights but the addresses are a long way from the area where he lives. He can't have a phone. I'm puzzled for a minute, then I remember Ryan was with the kids who followed Matthew home that time so I ring his number. His mother answers and it takes a few minutes for her to drag him to the phone.

'Robbie, why do you keep such uncivilized hours?'

'I won't keep you a minute. You can get back to dreamland as soon as you answer one question. Do you remember where Matthew lives?'

'Matthew again, I can't get away from the guy.'

'You seen him?'

'No, I heard some more of Luke's ranting and raving last night. It's getting around that Cassie's involved in it and Luke doesn't like the publicity. It's odd but they live quite close together. You know Luke's family house?'

Now I know that I have to see Matthew and warn him. Luke's clearly not going to forget about it all.

'Yeah, I went there for a party. You were with me, Ryan.'

'Really? My memory's going, must have been a good party. Matthew's only a couple of streets away, on Bellmarsh Crescent. You can't miss the house. It's right at the end, the last house before the common.'

'Cheers.'

'What you doing down there?'

'I just want a word with him.'

'Best of luck. I'll see you tonight. I'll have woken up by then.'

I put the phone down and check everything's turned off in the kitchen, then I lock up and head into town.

My town is a ring of streets and light industry surrounded by countryside. The high street cuts through the centre. The north side is more affluent than the south. In the north there's one area for the real executives, their country retreats with long driveways, heated swimming-pools and huge gardens. Most of the people I know live west, in the ocean of semi-detached housing and woodland. But Bellmarsh Crescent is down in the south of the town. I have to walk down the high street and take some turns into the back streets, past warehouses and tired pubs, the odd, desolate shop. This is the only work area in the town. There are no trees here. It's not as bad as a big city industrial area. There's none of the urban decay that you can find in London, the wasteland areas, streets covered in graffiti and rusting cars. My town is small and modern. Wherever you are you're only a few minutes' walk from the high street. But it feels very different in this part of the town from my own area. The houses are small, new red brick, packed into tight little culs-de-sac and crescents. There are some play areas for the kids, the earth drying out and cracking in the heat. It feels like a desperate brick campsite, somewhere you go if there's nowhere else that will take you. I hardly ever come down here.

Bellmarsh Crescent is the last street before the countryside takes over again. But you can't just walk into rolling fields and woodland like you can from my house. The crescent loops around to join back with the long main street that runs through the south of the town but it doesn't quite close the gap. Matthew's house is at the end, leaving a space about the width of two more houses, and here you should be able to walk out into the fields but there is a large wire fence to stop you. You can see trees and lawns through the diamond shapes of the steel net but you can't get out to them. On the other side of the fence the land is private, a golf course where executives unwind. None of the local kids are allowed on to it. There's a metal plaque on the fence, 'Trident Security – Do Not Enter'. I stand on the other side of the crescent, staring at his house for a few minutes. I'm apprehensive. Then I realize that Matthew might see me from a window and I feel stupid for being nervous. I cross the asphalt and knock on his door.

There's no answer from my first attempt so I knock harder. I hear a movement behind the door. There's a spyhole set in the middle of the door and I notice it go dark for a second. Then the door swings slowly open and Matthew's standing there.

'What are you doing here? How'd you know where I live?'

'We left the conversation up in the air. I thought I could have another go.'

He looks surprised. I ask myself how many others have knocked on this door recently.

'Can I come in?'

'Yeah.'

He steps away from the door and backs into the room. I follow him in.

It's the usual kitchen set-up: a fridge, a cooker, a work surface and a little table. A window in the back wall looks out across the garden. The room is tidy. There's a neat pile of plates by the sink. Matthew turns and walks through into the hall.

'Shut the door.'

I pull the kitchen door shut and follow him. We enter the living-room. There's a TV set, a coffee table and a brown suite. The furniture's old but it's been well maintained so it still looks all right. Matthew doesn't sit down. He stands in the centre of the room with his arms crossed.

'What do you want to say, Robbie?'

'I know about Cassie.'

'Is that it? This is not a good idea, you shouldn't have come here. I think you should go.'

'I need to talk for a minute.'

'We can meet somewhere if you want, but not here. She'll be back any minute and if she sees you she'll get upset.'

'Who will?'

'My mother. Look, I'll meet you somewhere, tonight.'

'I can't do it tonight.'

I hear the door bang in the kitchen. Matthew tightens, his whole body is suddenly tense.

'Upstairs! Now!'

He moves around me for the door. We step into the hall. There's a figure coming through from the kitchen. Matthew has his hand on my back, pushing me forward.

'Who's that? Who've you got there then?'

It's a woman. It must be his mother.

'I don't want any of those dirty little kids in my house, I told you, Matty.'

He's almost shoving me up the stairs. I hear her slump into the front room, then we're at the top of the stairs. Matthew steps over to one of the doors and takes out a key from a pocket in his shirt. The door has a thin padlock on it and he fumbles with it for a few seconds. Then he opens the door and I step into his room.

The rest of the house was tidy but Matthew's room is incredible. It takes me a moment to take it all in. The curtains are drawn back and sunlight is bouncing off the walls. The walls are painted a bright, brilliant white and the floorboards have been sanded so that they're an ivory colour. There is very little furniture: a simple wooden bed with a duvet and pillow neatly arranged, a small low bookcase and a desk and chair by the windows. On the desk I can see sheets of paper covered with neat handwriting. Everything is carefully arranged and orderly.

'Sit down on the bed.'

He goes over to the door and he locks us in.

'Do you have to do that?'

'If I don't she comes in. I don't like her coming into my room.'

'Why not?'

He doesn't answer me but sits down at the desk and tidies some of the papers away.

'I don't understand why you've come to see me, Robbie.'

'Because I've heard about Luke. Is it true that you've been writing to Cassie?'

'Despite the fact that it's none of your business I'll tell you. Yes, I have been writing to her.'

'And you're surprised Luke's after you?'

'I never said I was.'

I'm feeling strange now, chatting with him, being in his room. I've never associated him with an environment of his own, his own domain. It's obvious he doesn't like me being here. This is a place where there's no one to intrude, to remind him of the marks on his face. Now he's turned his head slightly to the wall. In the intense sunlight the scars are a bright purple and yellow weal on his skin.

'I've come round to warn you, to give you some advice.'

'What gives you the right to give me advice?'

'Because at least I care a little. I should have kept walking or done something back there in the woods, then it would have been clear, if I'd made a decision. I've been drifting ever since then, though. I'm not trying to come over as some kind of Samaritan . . .'

'A great guardian angel you'd make. You did nothing to help me.'

'. . . but I wanted to warn you about him. He's dangerous. I'm not talking about being your guardian. I didn't understand why it was happening and the more I think about it the more confused I get. I don't think you should be getting all this hassle, that's all.'

'I don't want your help. I've told you that. And I don't need your sympathy because of the way I look.'

I try to reassure him.

'It's not sympathy.'

'It sounds like it to me. I'll live my own life. If I have to then I'll fight Luke.'

'What did you mean when you said you didn't know if Cassie was "worth it", if it was worth fighting him?'

Now he sighs and looks down at the floor. He seems to be making up his mind whether to go on talking with me. Finally he looks up at me again.

'I don't know if she loves me.'

'You love Cassie?'

'I thought you knew about the letters?'

'But they were a joke, weren't they?'

'They were no joke.'

He stares at me, losing his usual nervousness about looking at you face-on. I've seen strength and determination in his eyes before and I see it again now.

'I love her. Luke doesn't think I've got any right to love his sister because of my face. It probably surprises you too, because you think I'm dreaming, that no one would want me, that I'd be crazy to think they would.'

'That's not true.'

'Well, it hadn't occurred to you, had it? I think she loves me but I'm not sure that's what I was talking about. If she wants me then I'll stand up to her brother.'

'He'll kill you.'

'I'm not as big as you but I've had to fight before. And this is something I want more than anything else. As I said, those letters were no joke.'

I've never heard someone my own age sounding so sincere about their feelings. When he says he loves her I know he means it.

'I haven't seen them, Matthew. But I don't understand why you'd write to her anyway, why not just . . .'

Then I see it all. I feel so clumsy, so ignorant. He's staring at the wall again. He wrote to her because of his face, because he wanted to approach her on an equal level to any other kid, not be judged by his face. The letters were a way in for him.

'You sent a lot of letters to her? She got to know you through your writing?'

'Yes. Then we finally started meeting. It was difficult the first time but she said something to me that gave me hope, it was so good hearing her say it. She said . . . imagine falling in love with someone so beautiful that you want to stare at them for ever but you truly love them, and then if that person and you were together in love and what happened to me . . .'

He reaches up and touches the side of his face with his thin white fingers.

'. . . if it happened to them, because of an accident or something, but your heart, what was in your heart, it wouldn't change, would it? That means that the love for someone is to do with so many different aspects of them other than just the way they look, it's almost nothing. No, no, it is important because it's like a triumph of your love, if the person you love is beautiful as well but it should be that way round, not beauty being the first thing that matters.'

He rushes the words out in a breathless stream, finishes with a sigh. I think he's crying because his eyes are moist but he's smiling; if he's crying it's with tears of joy.

'And when she said that, I knew that I had a chance with her. If I could have someone that strong in my life then I couldn't be sad. I've had to look after myself, I've become tough but I never lost hope, I never wanted to be one of those people that locked themselves away from the world, hated it in order to survive. That's what my mother does.

Why did you come here? I've got no one to talk to. I can't see Cassie now because of Luke, I've got no one. Why do you come round here when my defences are down and try to tear this out of me?'

'Matthew, I don't . . .'

'I can't trust you. I shouldn't have said all that stuff to you.'

'It goes no further than me. I'm glad you told me.'

I feel as though he's given away so much and there's nothing I can say in response. I let him down before, he's right. He can't rely on me. But listening to Matthew as he spoke just now I was tied to the spot, none of my friends have been so clear with their words, so honest about their feelings to me.

'Matthew, let's go out. Let's go for a walk.'

I want to get him out of the house, away from his mother and the pressure it must put him under. Looking around at this immaculate room I can guess that it's Matthew who keeps the rest of the house so clean. I can see him in my mind now, running back every night after school to clean up after her, to feed her, to help her in every way. I never thought that was why he wouldn't hang around with us at school but now I'm sure that's one of the reasons. I want to get him out just for an hour or two.

'A walk?'

'Yeah, we'll walk round to the high street and get a drink. We can talk a bit more.'

'Oh, I've talked so much already. Too much.'

'No, we're just beginning. Come on.'

'We'll have to be quiet. Really quiet.'

'I can be quiet. Come on, let's get out and get some air.'

We creep down the stairs and out of his house. I can hear the TV rumbling in the front room. His mother has pulled the door shut and blocked out the world.

'I can't be gone long. I have to make her something to eat.'

'We'll walk up the high street. Just half an hour, yeah?'

'All right.'

We come on to a street that leads through to the centre of the town and I carry on walking, but Matthew stops behind me.

'Let's go through this way instead, Robbie.'

'But this is quicker.'

'I want to go another way.'

'All right.'

I assume it might be something to do with Luke. I'm not sure where he lives but maybe his house is on the way up to the high street and Matthew's worried about bumping into him. We turn into a quiet road and Matthew leads me up an alleyway and back on to the high street. I start walking to a café.

'Let's go over to Albert's.'

'What's that?'

'You've never been in there? It's a café.'

'No, I haven't been into many cafés.'

'Come on. You've been missing out.'

There are people out shopping, bustling around town. I'm hoping there'll be no one I know in Albert's. I want a chance to talk with him alone and he may feel uncomfortable if I run into a friend. We push through the door and take a booth seat. Albert's is one of those pastiche American diners, with a long bar and lots of polished wood, with side booths where you can sit in some privacy. Matthew seizes the menu and studies it.

'I haven't got any money.'

'It's on me. What d'you want?'

'Just a cola.'

A girl comes over, takes our order and marches back to the bar to get our drinks. It's not very busy, I don't see anyone I recognize.

'You know my mother, don't you?'

'Yeah. We've met a few times but I haven't seen her for a while. That's the reason I'm talking with you now.'

'You what?'

'I figured that if you were her son you couldn't be all bad.'

It's the first thing he's said to me that has a trace of humour in it. I see a smile on his lips for a second then it disappears.

'Thanks for the compliment, Matthew.'

'She must have been talking to you about me. That's why you came round.'

'No, it was me who wanted to see you. I told her I'd seen you in the woods and she mentioned that she knew you, that's all.'

'She didn't tell you about my face, how it happened?'

'No. How did it happen?'

I don't want to anger him, to drive him away again, but I'm curious. He doesn't look bothered by my question. Our drinks arrive. He looks up at the waitress.

'Thanks.'

'You're welcome.'

She doesn't look at him, stares at the table, then walks away. He looks back at me.

'It was a fire, obviously. It was a house fire, five years ago.'

'I don't remember you at school back then.'

'That's because I wasn't there. We'd moved from another town. We were only here a few months before it happened.'

'Do you remember it?'

'I think about it a lot. It was a long time before I could think about anything else. It's not just my face. I lost my father in the fire.'

'I didn't know.'

'You thought it was just mum and me? No, he died when the house burned. He was away a lot. I think they were splitting up. I was there for some of the arguments. But he was there that day, when it happened.'

Matthew is looking down at the table, as though he's forgotten I'm here. His mind is going back to the time when his life changed for ever. He bears a permanent reminder of it on his face.

'But I don't want to say any more about it. That's in the past. Robbie, I want you to do something for me. I want you to give a message to Cassie. Since Luke found out that we were together I haven't been able to see her. I tried the other day but he was there, that was the day you saw me in the woods. He was outside the house with some of his meat-heads, his idiot friends from London. I tried to talk with him but he pushed me down and I ran. They chased me in a car, that's why I went to the woods, I didn't think they'd come after me there. I know he's determined to stop me but I'm not giving in. I've got to see her.'

'You want to be with Cassie that much?'

'There's nothing else, it's all I want, to be with her. Will you speak with her?'

'Of course. I should see her tonight. I think she'll be at a party I'm going to.'

'And you'll arrange a meeting?'

'If I can. I'll meet you tomorrow and let you know.'

'Thanks. You don't have to do it. If Luke finds out . . .'

I'm angry that Luke has this power over him. Not that Matthew is scared of him, it's just that he has to bear Luke in mind every time he makes a move. Luke shouldn't be allowed to be such an influence on him.

'Luke won't find out, and anyway he'll think twice about dealing with me.'

'Why are you siding with me, Robbie? I can't think of any reasons for it. Is it because of your mother?'

'I told you before, I felt bad that I didn't help. You should help anyone in distress, the way you were when I saw you. And after that I started thinking that we'd never had a chance to talk. It's easy to stick with one crowd at school and ignore everyone else.'

'That was never one of my problems, was it? Can I have another of these?'

He points at his glass. I've got my father's fifty-pound note in my jeans pocket. It makes me think of him and I realize how petty I was, coming back on the train cursing him, angry and frustrated after the day round at his flat. I could stand up and walk to a phone now, call him up and talk if I wanted to. Sometimes I think life's all about drawing straws, a game of chance. Matthew's experiences and my own are so different but it's nothing to do with the kind of people we are, how daring or intelligent or honest we might be. It could be me sitting there with the empty Coke glass, telling his story.

'I think I can afford it. I'll give the waitress a shout.'

83

'Do you see much of your father?'

He's studying me, as though he could tell what I was thinking a moment before.

'He's going abroad. I don't see him much.'

'So many people split up these days. It never used to be like that. They used to stick it out.'

'But they were probably unhappy. It's easier to do it these days, that's all. You don't have to live a lie.'

'Weren't you angry when they separated?'

'Yes, but it was because I didn't understand what was happening, I felt left out. I still get angry with him now and again, I can't help it. He was the one who broke it up. Most of the time it's all right. I do feel a lot closer to my mother though. Although it sounds crazy I think it was a good thing for her. It was the right thing to do.'

I catch sight of the waitress and order the drinks, then I turn back to him.

'You think people should stay together?'

'I'm not sure. Maybe they give up too easily sometimes. I was just saying how common it is.'

'Yeah. Married parents seem like the exception among my friends.'

'I have to get back.' His voice is suddenly anxious.

'Let's have the drinks first, I've ordered them.'

'No, I didn't know it was so late.'

He's gripping his watch, the muscles in his arms are tensed. His demeanour has changed. A second ago he was relaxed and chatty but now he's anxious. He stands up from the booth.

'Matthew!'

'I'm sorry about this. I really have to go. I've had a good time, I enjoyed talking. You will speak to Cassie, won't you?'

'I will, don't worry. When can we meet up tomorrow?'

'I can't get away till lunchtime. One o'clock. Down at the river, the little bridge near the station, d'you know it?'

'Yeah.'

'I'll be there at one o'clock. Thanks for having the drink with me, Robbie.'

It's the Matthew I used to know who leaves the café, shuffling quickly to the door and out into the street, nervous and agitated. I watch him cross the road and take a turn. I stare after him until I hear the waitress behind me.

'Is he coming back? We'll have a rush on in a minute and you're at a four-seater.'

'Sorry?'

'The table. Can I move you to another table?'

'No. Can you bring me the bill please?'

I finish the drinks, pay and head back to the high street.

Ruth's another west-side resident, living only a street or two from my place. The afternoon's dying but it will be light until nine o'clock, the sky's white, it's still hot. Ruth answers the door. She's wearing a thin cotton top that shows her belly and skin-tight jeans that could be straight from the bag they look so new. Her hair is pulled up at the back and she's wearing make-up. Some of the party preparations are obviously well under way.

'Hi, Robbie. Did you bring anything to drink? Sarah said you'd pick some stuff up.'

'I've been busy but I'll go out again in a minute.'

'Checking up on us are you? Come in.'

Sarah's in the living-room moving furniture back against the walls. I put my arms around her and kiss the back of her neck.

'Perfect timing, Robbie. I want the sofa out of here.'

'What a welcome.'

'Where've you been? Ruth and I have been waiting.'

'I'm here now. I haven't seen you for ages, can we vanish upstairs for a minute?'

Ruth's coming into the room behind me. 'Not a chance. Sarah's on party duty so you can smooch later.'

'What time are people coming round?'

'Soon. I've asked close friends around early then the rest are turning up at about nine.'

'So it's a staggered party, in stages?'

'Yeah, we've done some food for the honoured few.'

I want to spend some time with Sarah, it feels

like months since I've been with her. I know exactly who'll be in the early party. It'll be the usual clique from school, having the same conversations, making the same moves on each other they always have done. I want to talk in private with Sarah about Matthew, tell her it's genuine between him and Cassie. I'm not in the mood for the 'gathering', it felt fresh talking with Matthew, discovering someone new in town. I'm bored with the gang from school, we've been hanging out together all summer.

Sarah squeezes my hand and whispers into my ear. 'It's all set about tomorrow.'

Ruth grabs Sarah's arm. 'Hey, lovebirds, I need some help here. Robbie, sort the sofa out, will you?'

'Yes, boss.'

Sarah moves away, smiling at me. It's so good seeing her. After all the hassle seeing my dad and the events of today I've got so much to share with her. I feel lucky she's in my life, that I don't have to fight just to be with her. She walks over to the CD system and puts a dance track on. Ruth's next to her, fiddling with a lamp. The doorbell rings.

'I'll get it. The sofa's not going to run off anywhere.'

Ryan's out on the drive, holding a plastic bag that's bulging with beer cans.

'The booze man has arrived.'

He's wearing a shirt that has obviously been ironed.

'Ryan boy, you get your mum to sort you out with the threads then?'

I slap his arm with my hand.

'Don't say another word, Robbie. This could be a night of passion for me.'

'Who's the intended victim?'

'I cannot divulge such vital information but let's say I'm flexible.'

'I understand. Come on, you can help me with the furniture.'

'I knew I'd got here too early.'

We spend the next hour tidying the house, stripping it of anything that might get smashed. Ruth's parents have gone away for a weekend in London to celebrate their anniversary. In a mad moment of happiness they said she could have a party in their absence. She's got an older sister who's supposed to supervise, but as far as I can tell the sister's hiding away with her boyfriend whom she's not supposed to be seeing any more because the parents think he's too wild. It's the usual set-up for a party in my town. I think Ryan might be keen on Ruth. He probably thought Sarah and I wouldn't be here so early. He looks strange in an ironed shirt. He keeps tugging at the collar, as though he can't breathe properly.

The doorbell starts ringing every few minutes and soon there are about twenty guests milling around. Sarah and Ruth pass plates of snacks around, it's all very civilized. Ryan comes over to me with two cans of beer.

'Want one?'

'I'll have a glass. Let's go through to the kitchen.'

We walk through the crowd in the living-room. There's no one in the kitchen. I check in the cupboards and find a tumbler.

'Stick some in that.'

'Have a can. It's easier.'

'I'm not a hard-drinking man like you, Ryan. I'm pacing myself.'

'Yeah, each to their own. It should liven up in a while. Loads of people are coming. It's a bit of a dinner party atmosphere at the moment.'

'I agree.'

'How'd it go with Matthew? You go down to his house?'

'Yeah. We went out to Albert's.'

Ryan looks surprised.

'You actually had a conversation? I've never heard him say more than a word or two.'

'We had a good talk. I wish I'd got to know him at school a long time ago. He told me about Cassie, it's for real. And about some of his past. I like the guy.'

'Well, there are always two sides to any story, Robbie.'

'What do you mean?'

'Nothing. Have another glass. You've almost finished that one.'

'I haven't touched it, Ryan.'

The music is suddenly booming from the other room.

'Sounds like it's picking up a bit.'

We walk through to the living-room. Ruth's drawn the curtains and the table lamps are on. I'm amazed to see a few of the girls dancing in the centre of the room, Sarah included.

I turn to Ryan, who's leering at Ruth. 'I'm going out to get some drinks. Otherwise I might get grabbed for a dance. You want to come?'

'No. I've got a stash in the fridge already.'

I head back into the kitchen and out into the daylight.

Even though I've only had one glass of beer I feel light-headed. I'm not a big drinker. Ryan says it takes practice to start enjoying the taste. I head out into the street and walk down to the shops at the end. I'll get some soft drinks and maybe some cans of lager if Harvey's in a good mood.

Harvey runs a little grocery shop that also sells alcohol. He's middle-aged, very fat and has a shiny red nose. Some of the kids call him Rudolph. I've been visiting his shop for years and I often used to wonder about Harvey's behaviour because he shifted from elation to despair from one afternoon to another. Sometimes he wouldn't even look at you, just take your money and stare at the old-fashioned till he has on the counter. Then I'd duck in there the next day and he'd be smiling and telling jokes, positively radiant. It was only when I was around fifteen that I realized he was a drinker. He keeps a half-bottle of whisky under the counter. I caught him taking a nip once, opened the door and he had his head tilted back with the bottle to his lips.

After that I've tried to avoid him on the bad days, even glance through the window before entering. He's been getting worse lately. The shop closes for a day or two and nobody sees him around. Possibly he has contributed to my lack of enthusiasm for drinking. I don't want to end up like Harvey, using alcohol to deaden the pain. And I think of Matthew's mother, stumbling round the house, trapped in a dark world where the only solution is the very thing that might have put you there in the first place. Then there's my father. He says that drinking is part of his job and he can take it but I'm not sure. He's got enough money to protect himself from some of the pitfalls. He's not stuck in a corner shop like Harvey, wondering how he got there. All the same, the alcohol changes your mood and if you do it every day for years, for decades like my father, then it must start to shape your personality, the subtleties of your life, like the way you relate to people, your own opinion of yourself.

One day I might ask Harvey about his life. He may have had a fascinating youth, ending in some terrible trauma. Perhaps he sailed the seven seas and felt the loneliness of the ocean or was a test pilot and couldn't take the stress. He started relying on the bottle too much and retired to a shop for a hassle-free life. I suspect his past is more typical than that – divorce or redundancy leading to a breakdown and semi-retirement. There are people coping with the problems in their lives everywhere, however they can. I think about what people might be feeling all the time. Ryan thinks it's crazy. He says it's depressing to try and understand people who aren't directly important in your own life, thinks it's better to concentrate on the people close to you. But I've always been interested in everyone. Even though my town is tiny it's still full of a vast array of characters and stories. How can you get smart if you're not inquisitive? I know I could get on with Matthew now, that we could be friends. That would have been hidden from me if I hadn't made the effort to see him.

I check for signs of life through the window of Harvey's shop. He's standing at the counter, reading a newspaper. It looks safe to enter, he's not swaying around or anything.

'Hello.'

'Hello there.'

He gives me a smile, then goes back to the paper. I walk to the back of the store and take out some cartons of fruit juice from an open-fronted fridge. The booze shelves are next to it. I snake out a hand and grab a four-pack of the cheapest lager I can see, then walk boldly back to the counter. Harvey's so overweight he breathes loudly, trying to drag the air down into his lungs. He looks up at me.

'How are you?'

'I'm well.'

'Good. Good.'

He stretches out a meaty paw and selects a fruit juice carton to check the price. I wonder if he's asking himself how old I am. I could pass for eighteen but he's been seeing me around here for years, he must know I'm still at school. He studies the price tag and pushes some buttons on the till. He repeats this with the other juice boxes and finally reaches for the beer. He lifts it up to his face and I think for a second that he's going to say something but he's only looking at the bottom of the cans. For some reason, probably a drunken one, he's stuck the price sticker on the base.

'That everything?'

'Yeah.'

I pay him and watch him load the stuff into a tall brown paper bag.

'Be seeing you.'

'Goodbye.'

I walk out and pull the door behind me. There's no one in the street. He probably stands there for hours sometimes, waiting for a customer. The bottles are calling to him from the other end of the shop. I'll ask him about his life one day, find out what he thinks about all day long.

I stroll back to Ruth's house. I can hear the music clearly, out in the street. It sounds more of a party than when I left. That's good. If there's more of a crowd then I might be able to rescue Sarah from Ruth's clutches for a few minutes. I turn into the driveway and Cassie's standing at the back door, pressing hard on the doorbell.

I've spoken with her at school quite a lot but I don't know her as well as the girls that hang around with Sarah. She's popular but she spends most of her time with two other girls and they make a bit of a clique. She's wearing a blue cotton dress with her hair down over her shoulders. She's very pretty but not in the same way that Sarah is. Sarah's got the conventional 'model' looks, the thin, sexual style that the fashion press say is the way all women should look. Consequently, nearly every male thinks she is gorgeous because they've got the same expectations, I suppose. Cassie looks 'different'. I don't know anyone that looks anything like her and it's this uniqueness that makes her pretty. I walk over to her.

'Can't they hear you in there?'

'Hi, Robbie. No, I've been ringing for ages.'

'You have to wait for a gap in the music, between

the tracks.'

'I was about to go home. I wasn't sure about coming anyway.'

'Why's that?'

'It's not really my crowd. It was kind of Ruth to invite me but I was surprised she did.'

'Think of it as an opportunity to get to know them all.'

'We could have done that over the last year. How are you? Sorry, I sound sour, don't I? No, the other thing is, I think my brother's coming and we're not on the best of terms.'

'Because of Matthew?'

'Yeah.'

She stares at me, clearly perplexed I know anything about it. It seems as though she's thinking, 'Maybe Robbie's not such an idiot after all.' Cassie's very bright. She's quick to comment if she thinks someone's being dull. I've seen her savage guys if they're making sexist remarks. Maybe that's why some of the girls find her hard to get on with. They find her a little fierce.

'I've got a message for you. Let's go into the garden.'

'Top secret, is it?'

'It's a private message, that's all. From Matthew.'

We cut around the back of the house and lean against the wall. Ruth's garden is the usual square of grass with some struggling flowerbeds. There are some paving-stones at the back of the house and an old wooden bench. Cassie holds her dress in place and sits down.

'I didn't know you and Matthew were friends.'

'I've seen him a couple of times in the last few days, that's all. It took all this hassle with Luke for me to realize how stupid it was that I'd never spoken with him.'

'So you know about his letters to me?'

'Yeah.'

'Luke said he was going to pass them around but I didn't think he'd do it. Don't get me wrong. He's a spiteful jerk but I thought he'd be too ashamed. You should have heard him when he found out.'

'Didn't your folks say anything to him?'

'They're too busy watching TV and planning their next holiday. They gave up on me years ago. Luke does what he wants. I think he broke their faith in having children when he was younger. What's the message?'

'He wants to meet you tomorrow.'

She doesn't say anything.

'I said I'd help you to meet up.'

'How come you're so accommodating?'

'I'm just helping out. You can meet at my house if you want. You want to see him, don't you?'

'It's sad that we have to meet through you.'

'What do you mean?'

'Well, this is the first I know about you being some big friend of Matthew. And why should we have to creep around like this?'

I feel almost disappointed. I thought she'd be happy, that she'd been missing him and was desperate to see him.

'Are you in love with Matthew?'

'Is that beer in your bag?'

'Yeah.'

'Can I have a sip?'

'Sure.'

I get a can out and pop it for her. She holds it daintily, with two fingers, takes a long drink.

'I don't know, Robbie. Matthew's been asking me that over and over but I haven't spoken with anyone else about this, you know. It would be a big change. It's not like we can just start visiting each other, sitting in bedrooms, strolling hand in hand down the high street. I'd like some more time but there isn't any. Luke wants to kill him.'

I sit down next to her on the bench and take the can from her, take a drink. It tastes disgusting. I pass it back to her and lick my lips. It always tastes bad to me. Her expression has changed. She was being hostile at first, her usual tough approach, but now she's accepted that I'm being genuine, that I am all right to talk with.

'We've got no time. I know I want to see him but I can't be sure I'm ready for everything that would happen. He wants to go away. Do you know about that?'

'No. Where to?'

'London. He's going to get some kind of special

97

scholarship or something, because he's such a good student and writer. Have you seen his writing?'

'No.'

I remember the neat patterns of words across the papers on his desk. He had obviously spent hours working on each page. I wish I'd had the chance to read some of it.

'It's incredible, Robbie. He said everything in his letters, he'll walk the exams. He came top last year but he didn't tell anyone. He thought it would make him even more unpopular. If it had gone on like that then it might have been all right, but Luke came in and ruined it. Now we have to decide. He wants to get out with me, out of this town.'

'Don't you want to go?'

'I do but it's happened too quickly. And then there's the other things Luke's been saying . . .'

'What's that?'

'I can't tell you. It's too much for me to think about. I know my brother and I know what he's capable of. I don't want to believe him but he's got under my skin with it. And I can't ask Matthew. It's too painful for him to talk about.'

'I don't understand.'

'You'll hear about it. When Luke needs to spread it around he will. I wish he was back in London, that he hadn't come back. Matthew and I were going to spend the summer together, take it all gently. You can imagine the reaction if we'd just announced it, that we were an item. Can you see Matthew walking in here with me tonight?'

'Why not?'

'Because of the way they all are. Matthew's strong enough to take it but I'm not sure I am.'

I hadn't thought about the pressure she was under.

'He said you were very strong for him. That you were all he needed.'

'Oh, don't get me wrong, Robbie. I know Matthew and I want to be with him – well, I was sure before Luke said those things to me. No, I'm strong enough, but I get so angry at the way he's been treated, that's what I can't take.'

'You may have to get used to it.'

'That's what he says. But I'm so confused now.'

'What's Luke been saying?'

'I can't tell you.'

'You said he's coming tonight. Maybe I'll ask him.'

'Don't get into anything with Luke, please. It won't help and everyone will find out then.'

I want them at least to have a chance to work it out. They shouldn't feel persecuted like this, just because they want to be together.

'Will you see Matthew?'

'Is your number in the phone book?'

'Yeah.'

'I'll give you a ring in a day or two, Robbie.'

'I have to see Matthew tomorrow.'

'I'm sorry, I need more time. Look, I'm going home. I can't deal with this party, not tonight.'

She hands me the drink can and stands up.

'Robbie, thanks. I'm not sure you know what you're getting mixed up in but I think your heart's in the right place, so thank you. But don't think you can get to know Matthew in a couple of days. You only know a little about him. Don't let it wreck things for you. I have to go. I'll call you.'

I sit on the bench and try to drink some more of the beer. My thoughts are racing. This was supposed to be a summer of leisure, a long holiday with Sarah, but I seem to have stumbled into something too complex for me to understand. It's like a ring of fire. Every time I think I've reached the edge there's another obstacle for me to deal with. This time it's come back to Luke again. He knows something that has got Cassie scared, confused. I can hear people talking in the kitchen. I've been gone for a while now. I leave the beer unfinished and go round to the back door. Sarah's leaning out into the drive.

'I was about to send out a search party.'

'Sorry, I was taking my time.'

'Come on, we've got thirsty people in here.'

I kiss her on the cheek and step into the kitchen.

It's getting noisy now. In an hour it'll be chaos. Ryan looks as though he's been raiding his stash. He's red-faced and smiling, trying his best to squeeze in next to Ruth where she's dancing in the middle of the carpet. She's with Morgan, the school sports hero. I don't think Ryan's in with a chance. Ruth is staring at Morgan as though he's a perfect physical specimen of manhood, which he is. He's got nothing to say, though. Conversations with Morgan rarely make it past the 'hello', 'good-bye' level. Some of his friends are hugging the walls, staring across at the girls on the sofa, huddling around the sound system. There's a house track blaring. Nearly everyone from my year at school seems to be here. Ruth's tried her best to make the room look like a club, she's even replaced some of the standard light bulbs with red- and blue-toned ones. But it's still her living-room. She can't change that.

Sarah pulls me into the throng. I notice Peter and Ralph, Zack and his girlfriend. I nod hello to a few people. I can understand what Cassie was getting at though. I know these people, I can have a trivial, mildly amusing chat with them, but I don't feel as though they're my good friends, except Ryan, of course. Sarah's buzzing, the party has got her excited. She can drop into a conversation, make a remark and get everyone laughing, then move on to the next group. She knows them all, the relevant 'girlfriend/boyfriend' details, who's doing what. She's a socialite. She loves the noise and the talk. But as far as I can tell, not much of any interest is being said. There's lots of beer and cider in the room, a cheap bottle of supermarket vodka sitting on the mantelpiece. Only a few people are smoking, but because the curtains are shut and there's no air coming through the open windows the room is smoky. I grab hold of Sarah and I can smell the smoke in her hair.

'Let's get some air for a second.'

'It's just starting.'

'A second, that's all.'

'All right.'

She waves farewell to someone and then we spin out of the room. I was going to head for the garden but she steps over to the stairs.

'Ruth's room's free.'

'What, you mean some people have made reservations?'

'Could be. It'll be mayhem up here later.'

We head up the stairs holding hands. Ruth's door is open.

'We can't be long, Robbie.'

She pulls me on to the bed and kisses me in a frenzy of lips and arms as we tumble across the sheets. I can taste wine on her lips.

'Hey, calm down.'

She's making me laugh, almost tickling me.

'I thought you'd run off with Cassie.'

'You saw her?'

'Yeah. What were you talking about back there? Don't tell me, I can guess. Matthew getting a mention again?'

'I met up with him.'

She pulls back slightly and brushes the hair from her eyes.

'Why didn't you say earlier?'

'This is the first chance I've had to say anything. You were busy with Ruth.'

'How'd it go?'

'Great. We get on, I think.'

'If you'd told me I would have come with you. I know you've been thinking about it a lot – well, I want to know what's on your mind all the time, Robbie. I want this to be a proper relationship.'

Her words are slightly slurred.

'How much wine have you had?'

'Don't be like that with me. It's a party, isn't it? I'm being serious anyway.'

'All right. That's good. I don't mean to give you a hard time about Matthew, there's no reason for you to turn up and see him on my account, but maybe we could all go out one day. I'm glad you said that, we haven't been talking a great deal, have we, in the last few weeks?'

'Are you unhappy?'

'No, I want to be with you. Don't be crazy. Why d'you think I dragged you up here?'

'Kiss me then.'

'So your father's flat's free?'

'Yes. I'm going to make you an amazing lunch and we can spend the whole day together, with no interruptions.'

'I'm busy in the morning. Can I meet you there at lunch?'

'One o'clock. And don't keep me waiting.'

She kisses me again. When I feel her I usually forget everything else but here in Ruth's house I can still hear the music and talk downstairs, I'm still thinking about what Cassie was saying, the secret her brother has that taunts her. It's the first time I've not focused only on Sarah when we kiss and it makes me feel worried. I need to spend some time with her tomorrow and sort it out.

'Let's go down to the party, Sarah.'

'All right. I'll wander over and see how you are every now and again. Don't forget me.'

'I won't.'

I lose her in the crowd and go in search of Ryan. He's sitting in the kitchen with Wilbur.

'Hey, Wilbur.'

'All right, Robbie.'

Wilbur's in the year below us but he hangs around with Ryan a lot. He's a comedian, always pulling stunts and clowning around. He's small, with short blond hair. He's dressed in beach-bum gear and a baseball cap.

'Ryan's been pouring his heart out to me. He's a spurned lover.'

'You didn't pounce, did you, Ryan?'

Ryan's draining a can of beer. He looks miserable.

'I didn't have the nerve. I asked her in a round-about way.'

'Like how?'

'I asked her if I could get her a drink and she told me Morgan was "in control of that".'

'Bad luck. The shirt didn't work then?'

It looked immaculate a few hours ago but now it's creased and stained with splotches of beer and other unidentifiable liquids.

'She's made a terrible mistake.'

Wilbur lifts a plastic bag on to the table.

'Have a drink and cheer yourself up.'

'What is it?'

'Sherry. I stole it from my dad's cabinet.'

'Paint-stripper.'

'It'll make you feel better. Robbie?'

'I'll pass. Thanks anyway.'

We sit at the table and they start guzzling the sherry. I have to open the door occasionally to let new people in. Soon the party's spilling into the kitchen and Ryan and Wilbur decide to retreat to the garden with the bottle. I turn back to the living-room to look for Sarah but the doorbell goes. Luke's standing in the driveway with some of his London friends.

'Thank you, doorman.'

He pushes past me and into the room. I stand aside for his friends. Luke's wearing a denim jacket and jeans. His skin is damp, his eyes look tired, but he is as brash as ever.

'How's it going, Robbie boy? We almost caught up with your friend after you left, scar-face ran off like a frightened cat though.'

'I saw it all. I saw him climb out of the gully.'

Luke has a certain cunning despite the fact he's stupid. He checks my face to try and tell what I'm thinking.

'Is my sister here?'

'No. She left hours ago.'

'Here, pass it around.'

He pulls a bottle out from his jacket and throws it to one of his sidekicks. Then he leans in close to me, slips his arm over my shoulder and walks me into the hall. I can smell smoke and alcohol on his breath, he's so close.

'She tell you what's been going on?'

'I heard.'

'The guy's vermin. I'm going to track him down. But I don't want to spoil the party with my problems. Is the lovely Sarah here?'

He walks through to the living-room with me following. The music's louder than ever and some of the lights have been turned off so the room is a dark mass of weaving bodies in the sound. Luke pulls out a cigarette and lights it. I can see his face in the white glare from the lighter. His eyes look glazed, the skin is drawn tight across his cheekbones as he inhales. As they spot him people start to come over and meet him. Luke's popular even though he's a psychopath. He's never dull. His friends come through with the bottle and pass it to him. Sarah emerges from the mass of people and stands by my side.

'I was hoping he wouldn't show up.'

'He's the man of the party. They're all impressed.'

Luke's shouting and waving the bottle in the air. He charges into the crowd and takes Ruth's hand, dragging her from Morgan. Morgan just smiles. I expect Ruth to look shocked but she starts dancing with Luke, moving close to him. Luke sways like a drunk to the beat, the bottle in one hand, with the cigarette stuck between the fingers, the other hand pulling Ruth towards him. Sarah takes my arm.

'He's out of his head.'

'I know.'

Maybe with Luke like this Matthew might stand a chance if they come to fight. But I've seen Luke at parties before. He can go all night. He can snap out of the trance in a flash if he has to. I've seen the light come back into his eyes when he senses that something's about to happen, that he's pushed someone too far. I've seen him crouch low and move in on his victim.

My hands are clenched into fists. I feel very hot, can taste a drop of sweat on my lips that's fallen from my brow. I don't want Luke tackling Matthew. I could stop him now, at this party. I don't know if his friends would step in or not. But I had my chance earlier this week. I could have done something then. I can't just walk over and start it. That's the kind of thing Luke would do.

'Robbie, let's go to the kitchen. I need some juice.'

'Sure.'

The kitchen's almost as full as the living-room. People are moving out into the driveway and the garden, it's so packed in the house. We start talking with some of the kitchen crew. Sarah drinks two glasses of orange juice then starts back on the wine. It's dark outside now. I can see the shapes in the garden, couples looking for some privacy, kneeling circles of smokers. We manage to get a seat and Sarah sits on my lap. Ryan and Wilbur crash into the room looking blasted. Wilbur's finding it difficult to stand up.

'Make some room. Call an ambulance. Send up a flare.'

'Relax, Wilbur. You can chuck in the garden if you're desperate.'

'A Wilbur never chucks.'

He goes into one of his routines, an anecdote from the last year at school. Everyone's laughing. Luke comes stumbling out of the living-room.

'Sarah! A pleasure to see you again.'

He's leaning against the kitchen door. His eyes are half-closed, his words are slurred.

'Care to dance?'

I answer him.

'She's sitting this one out, Luke.'

108

'With the new boyfriend? I don't mean dancing here, Sarah. We're driving into town. Going to a club. I thought you might fancy a change of mood.'

'No thanks, Luke.'

'Suit yourself. I'll be seeing you. Get out of my way, jerk.'

Luke moves forward and pushes Wilbur across the room. Wilbur jumps up but when he sees who it is he stands still. Luke lifts his arm and points at him.

'That's right. You do what you're told like a good boy.'

He's stepping forward towards Wilbur. I can't take it any more. All I see is Luke pushing people around and no one doing anything to stop him. I lift Sarah off me and cross the room.

'Don't touch him, Luke.'

Luke turns slowly to face me. He's so smashed he can't stand up straight, he's slumped, loose-legged.

'Every time I start something you stick your pitch in, don't you, Robbie?'

'Just go.'

'It's going to take more than you to throw me out of a party.'

'Get out. And a word of warning.'

'You're warning me?'

He puts his head back and laughs. I can see he's coming around, his eyes are clearing. He's got the scent of some action. He's preparing himself, pulling himself together.

'Matthew might not be as all alone as you think.'

'Oh, no, he's all alone. All alone, you hear me? You saying you're backing him up? You're a fool. You don't know anything about it.'

'I know a lot about it. I know you're trying to keep him from seeing Cassie.'

'But you don't know why.'

'You haven't disguised that.'

'You mean the face, the funny face he's got? You think that's all it is?'

I can hear the music from the other room, all the talking and the noise. The house is vibrating with the party. But it feels as though there's no one else here except me and Luke. He's very close to me. I never thought I'd take him on like this. Sarah is saying something but I can't make out the words.

'Yeah, the scar.'

'That's only one part of it. It's true that I think he should have been put down because of it. No one that ugly should be walking the streets, scaring old ladies.'

He starts laughing again. He's so calm, while I can't remember ever being so tense.

'But no, there's more, a lot more about him that makes him scum.'

'Stop it, Luke.'

'I can prove it to you. I can show you the truth. If you can face it. Your tidy little ideas about Matthew will all be crushed, boy.'

'I don't believe you.'

'We shouldn't be fighting over him, Robbie. I'm not in the mood for it tonight anyway, feeling mellow tonight. I just want to head out to a club and relax. See me this week and I'll show you how wrong you are about him. I'll come round and get you.'

'All right.'

'I won't be getting up till the evening tomorrow and I've got some business in town. Be home the day after, round four. I know where you live.'

'I'll be there.'

'Sure you won't change your mind about tonight, Sarah, a bit of action?'

She doesn't answer him. He breaks out with his thin laugh again and heads for the door. I feel someone move behind me and turn. It's his friends. They were standing behind me the whole time. They smile at me as they file past.

'Robbie, how could you do that?'

She's tugging on my arm. As soon as Luke has left it's as though none of it happened. The party is still crashing along. Wilbur starts chatting. Sarah's shouting at me.

'What a mad thing to do!'

'I have to find out what he was talking about.'

'And what if he drives you out into the country? I might be spending the next month sitting by your bed in the hospital.'

'Nothing's going to happen. Relax.'

'This thing with Matthew is going too far. You shouldn't be putting yourself on the line for him like this. You're going to get hurt.'

'I have to find out what Luke's up to. It'll be all right. Hey.'

I put my arms around her. She's trembling.

'It'll be all right. Don't worry.'

After another hour the party starts to die out. Ruth turns the music down so the neighbours won't come round to complain, and that's the signal for people to think about going home. Sarah's angry with me but I promise her we'll have the afternoon together, that we'll have some time to talk. It's not far from where I'm meeting Matthew to her father's flat, only a minute's walk, so I should be too late. Ryan comes over to me, obviously smashed, and puts his head on my shoulder.

'Robbie, I'm not the man I used to be. I'm depressed.'

'You're drunk. How are you getting home?'

'I'll sleep in the garden. It's nice and soft on the grass.'

Sarah takes my hand. 'Lori's getting a cab back to her place. I can go with her.'

'Are you sure?'

'Yeah. I'll see you tomorrow. I'll be waiting. Lunch at one, all right?'

'Say thanks to Ruth for me. Great party.'

She gives me a smile, noting my sarcasm. She

looks stronger, as though she's made up her mind to stand by me.

'Ryan, can you walk?'

'Not in a straight line.'

'We'll have to swerve back to your house then.'

I kiss Sarah and drag Ryan over to the back door.

It takes about ten minutes to navigate him back to his house. During this time he's babbling about Ruth and praising me for stopping Luke's potential battering of Wilbur. He's not making much sense. When we get to his house the lights are still on. It's around midnight.

'I don't like the look of that, Ryan.'

'The inquisition awaits.'

It's the only house in his street that shows any sign of life. We stand for a moment underneath the orange stain of a streetlight set into the pavement.

'Can you make it to the door?'

He's got an arm around me, holding himself up. He breaks away, but his knees start to wobble so I grab hold of him again.

'Looks like I have to take you in.'

We cross the street and start up his driveway. As we approach the back door a light flicks on in the kitchen. Suddenly, in the new flood of light I can see his face in detail. He looks very sick, a yellow, sweating face.

'God, Ryan. Have you got a key? Get a grip, will you.'

The door swings open. His father stares at me, looking bored.

'In you come, Ryan.'

I expected him to be furious but his voice is soft.

'Thanks for getting him home, Robbie. I've got him now.

He takes Ryan round the waist and lifts him gently into the kitchen.

'Good-night.'

I march back to my house, thinking Ryan's very lucky to have a father who waits up for him and doesn't shout when he's late in. It reminds me that I have to call my own father. He'll be leaving soon. I let myself into my house and take the stairs to my room. I undress and stretch out on my bed, pensive in the darkness all around me. I'm a little nervous, almost excited. I want to know what Luke was talking about. I stood up to him. It feels good knowing I was prepared to do that and I'm going to see it through to the end.

Chapter 5

I should have left a note for her on the table telling her I'd got back all right. She's banging on my door and I'm so tired it's an effort to sit up in the bed and shout.

'Come in.'

'I brought you some tea.'

'Mum, what are you going to do with the tea if one day you come in to see me and I'm not here?'

'I like to check on you, that's all. Let's hope that day never comes.'

'It will do eventually. Thanks.'

'I give you so much freedom, Robbie. As long as I know you're back safely I don't mind. You shouldn't complain.'

'You think there's a risk I might get snatched? The white slave trade is rampant round here, is it?'

'It's not much to ask. You get a cup of tea out of it anyway.'

'I'm only joking, Mum. Thanks.'

'How was the party?'

'The usual jet set doing the usual things. It was all right.'

'You seem a bit "seen it, done it". You're too young to be jaded, surely?'

'I could do with a change.'

'Well, you'll have that in the autumn, won't you? You're thinking about going to London, I know you are.'

I haven't discussed it with her before. I'm surprised she knows I've been thinking about it. She senses this.

'It was fairly obvious. I didn't expect you to find this town fascinating for ever.'

'You wouldn't mind?'

'No, of course not. Did you ask your father about staying in his flat?'

'He's renting it out.'

'I should have guessed. So, what will you do?'

'There's some talk about renting a house but I haven't made my mind up about going yet. I might stay on and get a job here. I can always go up to London and visit for weekends and stuff.'

'Are you thinking about Sarah? Doesn't she want to go?'

'She's happy here. I think she'll make the break when she goes to uni.'

My mother stares at me, she looks pensive. I can tell she's worried that I'm too influenced by Sarah.

'I think it would be a mistake to stay here just

because of her. As you were saying, London's close enough for her to visit.'

'I don't believe in that long-distance relationship idea. You end up seeing other people, having nothing in common with each other.'

'Maybe, but if you don't go you may end up blaming her. You've got lots of time to think it over anyway, all summer.'

'How did you know I was considering London anyway, apart from assuming it, I mean?'

'Mothers form a very reliable information network. Don't you think we get together and talk? Anyway, I could see you were working hard for the exams so I knew you were up to something.'

I always forget how perceptive she is.

'What's the news with Jeff?'

'The news is that we're meeting for dinner again. Who knows, if I can get you out of the way this autumn I'll have the whole house for Jeff and me.'

'Hey!'

'Relax, Robbie. You'll always have this room to come back to if you do decide to go.'

'At least one of my parents is providing some stability then.'

'Well, your father helped. He bought this house after all.'

'I know, but it's only money.'

'Don't underestimate the stability of money. Anyway, you're talking to me as though I'm an old

117

age pensioner. I'm still young at heart. You can rely on the room but I might be travelling the world, off enjoying my youth.'

'With the maestro?'

'Maybe. He's asked me to go and see him play.'

'Where's that?'

'Brighton.'

'Not exactly glamorous.'

'First Brighton, next the world.'

She's laughing, I can see how happy she is with Jeff.

'Send me a postcard. Thanks for the tea.'

I'm passing her the empty mug.

'This isn't a hotel. You can take that down and wash it yourself. And while you're at it, the kitchen's a mess. I'd appreciate you giving it a quick tidy-up. I have to get going.'

'I'll see you tonight.'

'Have you rung your father? Have you said goodbye?'

'No. Not since I saw him.'

'I think he's going tomorrow.'

'I'll do it tonight.'

'What about Matthew? Did you talk with him?'

'Yeah, we're getting on all right. I'm seeing him later.'

'He'd make a good friend, Robbie. But he's not easy to get to know.'

'I gathered that.'

'He's worth the effort. See you later.'

She shuts the door behind her and I hear her leave the house. I get up to shut my curtains and slink back into bed.

It takes me a while to feel human again after I wake up. My throat feels dry and my eyes are sore. It's eleven according to my watch. I'm staring at the ceiling thinking about the afternoon with Sarah when I hear the telephone whining downstairs. From previous experience I know it's too far away for me to get there before they ring off so I take my time, get dressed, grab the mug and go down to the kitchen. I drop the mug in the washing-up bowl and turn the taps on, then cross to the phone and trigger the 'one-four-seven-one' function, a great invention for lazy telephone users. The voice gives me the number that's just called. I don't recognize it but I punch the 'respond' code button anyway. Live dangerously.

'Hello.'

It's Cassie.

'Robbie here.'

'I've tried you a few times already this morning.'

'The party went on a bit late.'

'I can't talk long. The house is packed. I want to meet him.'

'I'm seeing him at one o'clock. Do you want to come along?'

'No, I'm working today, I can't get out of it and Luke's circling like a vulture anyway.'

'What about tonight?'

'I doubt if Matthew could get out in the evening. Tomorrow morning would be better.'

'All right. I'll speak to him.'

'Are you meeting him at the bridge?'

'Yeah.'

'That's where we always met. I don't think it's a good idea to do it in town though, not at the moment. I'll be out at Saracen Hill at ten.'

'I know it.'

'I'll wait for half an hour. Thanks, Robbie.'

'No problem.'

She hangs up. It's a bit like an espionage movie, the coded message, the meeting place. Saracen Hill is a few miles out of town, a huge earth mound topped with a small copse of windswept trees. It's a historical site. We used to go out there on geography field trips from school. I go back to the sink and start scrubbing the dishes and cutlery that's accumulated over the last day or two. Most of it's mine. By the time I've cleaned up the kitchen and gulped a bowl of cereal it's time to meet Matthew. I lock up and walk towards the high street, blinking in the sunlight.

Even though I've got Luke to deal with tomorrow I feel on top of things. I've got it under control. Matthew's going to meet Cassie and they can have some time together. Luke's probably just being cagey, trying to confuse me. All the same, if he'd wanted to start anything he could have done it at the party, so he must have something to say. The town's busy but the crowds thin out as I near the river. It's more of a stream than a river, a murky brown trail through the town, hidden by buildings and the undergrowth along its banks. I cut past the station and take some crumbling brick steps down to the river path. It's shaded but still sweltering by the river. Along this part of the path there are houses on one side, their gardens coming down to the water and a long wall covered in creepers and bushes on my side. There's a thin mud path up to the bridge, it's baked and hard. The bridge is in the shadows of a small factory. It's just a little foot-bridge covered in graffiti scrawl. Matthew's sitting on the river-bank underneath it.

'Hi.'

My voice booms in the arch of the bridge. It's almost dark here in the shade.

'Hi, Robbie.'

I look down at him. His cheeks are wet with tears.

'What's got into you?'

'I've had a bad morning. That's all. Some days are worse than others.'

I can't remember the last time I cried. It's years ago, on some playing field or crashing off my bike, back in London, some misty image of me in my room, eyes stinging with the salt in the tears.

'What happened?'

'Nothing. Sometimes I have bad dreams. Did you speak with her?'

'Yeah, I saw her at the party. She didn't stick around. She was thinking about you.'

'Do you want to go for a drink? I got some money. I can buy you one. My turn.'

'No. I've got to see Sarah, I'm supposed to be around there now. Don't you want to hear about Cassie?'

'I thought we could do something this afternoon. Go out, you know.'

Going to Albert's was a big deal for him. I take so much for granted about my lifestyle. What I think is dull and typical is something new for him.

'I would have done, gone out with you somewhere, but I have to see her. I haven't seen much of her lately.'

'Are you really into her?'

'Yeah, I think so. We still don't know each other that well, I suppose. I thought we did but we've only been together a couple of weeks and it's different from how I thought it would be. I need to spend some time with her.'

I'm almost apologizing to him for not being around this afternoon. It makes me feel uneasy.

'Let's get back to Cassie.'

'Sorry, Robbie. I thought when you said we were going to meet it would be for a while, that's all. I didn't realize. Sorry.'

'Forget it. She wants to meet you tomorrow morning. Ten o'clock.'

'Will you come with me?'

'You what?'

He seems to have lost the little confidence he has shown me in the last few days. He looks close to more tears.

'Come along with me to meet her, Robbie.'

'She wants to see you on her own, though.'

'Did she say that?'

'No, not exactly.'

'I think she'd like someone else to be there. Why don't you bring Sarah?'

This is turning into a family outing. I don't know if he's trying to get my sympathy, if he's afraid of seeing her. He sounds so different.

'I hadn't thought about it. Anyway I have to get back to see Luke in the afternoon.'

'Luke?'

I wasn't going to tell him about it. I thought it would be better if I sorted it out on my own and let him know later. I didn't want to sound big-headed. But I want him to know what I've been doing for him. He needs some reassurance.

'Yeah. We had a bit of a showdown last night. He came out with some story, said he knew something else about you that might change my mind about you, so I challenged him. I'm going to see him and once this game's over he might leave you and Cassie alone.'

'I don't think it's a good idea.'

'But he's getting away with it, Matthew – some-one needs to shut him up.'

'I told you, I'll handle Luke.'

'You're not up to it, Matthew. He'd rip you up into little pieces.'

'And you're the big man who's going to work out all my problems, are you?'

He stands up, moves close to me. He looks angry, as though he's suddenly woken up out of the sad trance he was in.

'You only know me for a few days and you're fighting it out for me. That's not the way to be a friend, Robbie. I'm not some pathetic kid. I told you, I'll fight Luke if I have to. That's why I want you along tomorrow, I want your *support*, not your sympathy and your muscle. You don't have to see Luke for me.'

'I want to see him. Nothing's going to happen. I want to stop him shooting his mouth off, that's all.'

I thought this would be so easy, just deliver my message and go along to Sarah's. Matthew looks tense; he moves back towards the river.

'Just some simple support, that's all I ask. It's going to be difficult with her tomorrow, she has to make her mind up. I'd like to have someone there with me. I don't want you to fight my battles. I want your friendship. If you have to see Luke then there'll still be time anyway, you can be back by lunchtime. He's just going to tell you some more lies anyway. How do you think it feels, being debated like this, some kind of cause for people to argue over. I just want Cassie and to have a friend.'

'I think we are friends, or could be in time anyway.'

'Come along tomorrow then.'

'I'll ask Sarah. If she agrees then I'll come. I will see Luke though.'

'Whatever you want. But be careful, Robbie, you hardly know me, he'll try to trick you and you won't have any real knowledge of me to fall back on. He'll try to get you hating me.'

'I know Luke, don't worry. Tomorrow then. She'll be up on Saracen Hill. If we're coming we'll be at the station at half-nine but I'm not promising.'

'I might ask for your support again some time, Robbie. It depends on what she says. Will you be there then? Maybe you'll lose interest, stop thinking it matters.'

'Relax, Matthew. If you're straight with me you can count on my support.'

'Thanks. You'd better hurry. I don't want her to get mad with you because of me.'

'I might see you tomorrow.'

'I hope so.'

I turn and start walking back down the path to the steps. When I get to the end I look back. He's sitting on the river-bank again, staring into the water. I can imagine him sitting there for hours, until it gets dark and he can creep back to his house out of sight, under the cover of night. I feel like I should stay but I want to see Sarah. I will support him. There's lots of time. I decide to try and talk Sarah into the expedition.

She's out on the balcony when I get up to the flat. She lets me in by the intercom. I've rushed over, I'm out of breath.

'Your punctuality is on the slide, Robbie.'

'Sorry, I got held up.'

'Are you hungry?'

'Starving.'

'I've made a huge lunch, which is quite an achievement seeing how bad I felt this morning.'

'The wine? I didn't think you had that much.'

'Only three glasses. I think it was a bit rough.'

'That's what they all say.'

She goes back into the living-room and through to the kitchen. The flat is full of light. It's got cream carpets and walls, white furniture. It's the sort of place my father would live in. His flat in Singapore might be like this – modern, stylish but essentially lacking in any character. Anyone could live here. It feels like a hotel room. She starts bringing plates and bowls from the kitchen and laying them out on the coffee table.

'Can I help?'

'Please.'

I join her in the kitchen. It's white again, with chrome cooker and sink. It feels strange preparing the lunch with her, as though we're a married couple. This is so different from sitting on the edge of her bed in her house, listening for the parents coming in downstairs, hearing the noises her sister makes in her room.

We kiss for a moment then sit down and eat. When we finish I curl up on the sofa with her. She kicks her shoes off then twists around and fiddles with my trainers, pulling them off and throwing them into the corner of the room.

'Let's not talk about anything or anyone outside this room, Robbie.'

'Are you tired of the world?'

'This is a big enough world for me right now.'

'I know what you mean. All right, it's a deal if I can say one thing.'

'I don't know. I'm not sure that's allowed. Let's forget about everything.'

'Just one thing.'

'All right.'

'How'd you fancy going out to the country tomorrow?'

'Great.'

'With Cassie and Matthew?'

I think she's going to get mad but she kisses me and lays her head on my shoulder.

'You've been seeing Matthew a lot. I guess if you get on with him then I should. It's right what you were saying. Everyone did ignore him at school. I'd like to meet him. I get on with Cassie, although she thinks I'm an airhead.'

'She doesn't.'

'She does. She's always on someone's case, moaning. She thinks I'm stupid because I just want to have a good time.'

'Then it's her that's stupid.'

'But I'd like to come along.'

'Right, that's it then, no more outside world from now on.'

'You don't know how much I like you, Robbie.'

'Tell me.'

'You were always the quiet guy who made a lot of sense, who really thought about what you were saying.'

'It helps.'

'I mean it. I've been out with so many guys who just hassled me to sleep with them as soon as we were going steady but you seemed interested in me for real. What you're doing with Matthew is just one part of it. There's been a lot of talk about you hanging out with him but you're brave enough to stick with your convictions.'

'I'm not used to all this flattery.'

'And I want us to get to know each other. I want to find out about you.'

I kiss her, stroke her hair.

I had a friend at school who was a few years above me. He moved to London a while ago. I remember him telling me about these afternoons, telling me they would come my way some time, being locked away from the world with a girl you care about. He

128

told me that there was nothing else like it, that it was something you should treasure. The first few weeks are the best, when you're still happy just being in the same room, when you're blissfully content without having to do anything. Nothing concerns you, nothing can disturb you. You want to find out the way she moves, the way she holds a fork, crazy stuff like that. Magic afternoons that you think will last for ever but soon they're gone and you never get them back. He told me it only happens with one or two girls and then you're hardened, you expect it to happen with the next girl, force it and by doing that it is wrecked. It's like some kind of innocence, utter contentment just being in each other's arms, just touching.

I want it to go further with Sarah. I always watched her from a distance, wondering what she was like, thinking I knew about her. But I'm discovering new things about her every time I see her. I'm not going to forget this. I want all of her but I'm not going to push it. I'm so happy like this with her and each new visit to this flat leads to a new touch, a new degree of intimacy discovered. I want to keep coming here with her.

Some time in the evening I walk her home and wander back to my house. I can still taste her on my lips.

Chapter 6

Despite the fact I was walking on air when I got in, I remembered to leave a note out, so my mother doesn't wake me. When I open my eyes and check my watch it's nine o'clock. I've only got minutes to get down to the station. I pull on some clothes and race out of the house. It's not warm yet and I wish I'd brought my jacket with me. The town is still waking up, the shops are just opening. I jog down the high street and turn into the station car-park then cut through to the ticket office. Matthew and Sarah are standing by a coffee stand, trying to talk with each other with little success. Matthew's looking at the tarmac of the ticket hall, the cigarette butts and trash that cover it. Sarah is staring at the back of his head. They both look relieved to see me. Sarah hugs me and gives me a lingering kiss, whispers in my ear.

'I couldn't stop thinking about you last night.'

Matthew looks embarrassed and impatient to be going.

'We got you a ticket.'

'Sorry I'm late. When did you two get here?'

'Only a minute ago. Matthew was here before I was.'

'Well, I always make the train, perfect timing. It should be here in a minute.'

We buy some coffees and go out to the platform. Sarah looks slightly perplexed but she's trying to keep a conversation going with him.

'I wonder why Cassie didn't meet us at the station.'

'She'll be on her bike. She's got a mountain bike.'

'Right.'

I try and lighten the tension between them.

'No picnic, Sarah?'

'No chance. There's a restaurant in the village. I thought we could go there for lunch. On you.'

'Oh, yeah? I owe you one, I guess.'

I've got most of the fifty left. Harvey's lager is very cheap – no surprise considering how it tastes. I pass Matthew a few pounds.

'For the ticket.'

'Don't worry about it.'

'Take it.'

He puts the money in the pocket of his jeans. They're the ones he always wears but he's in a shirt I haven't seen before, loose denim, a bit smarter than usual. He's in the normal trainers, falling to bits. Sarah's dressed up as always but she's not wearing make-up. I think she looks better without it, fresher. The tain pulls in to the platform.

'It's a relic.'

'This isn't the London line, this is where old trains come to die.'

'Does it run on steam?'

'Quiet, you'll hurt its feelings.'

We pull the doors open and climb in. The seats are covered in the dirty-blue patterned fabric of old trains. The carriage smells musty. Sarah starts coughing.

'Open one of the windows, will you, Matthew?'

He's standing next to the door. He flips his hand under the window sill. I step over because I think he might need a hand. The windows are stiff on these trains. But Matthew lifts it easily.

'You're stronger than you look.'

'I have my moments.'

We pull out of the station, gazing at the green countryside and sipping our coffee. As we get away from the town the conversation starts to flow. We're the only ones in the carriage and we're making a lot of noise, messing around. A fat guard comes round to check our tickets. Matthew calls to him as he leaves.

'Which way's the restaurant car? And the casino?'

The guard gives him a scowl and staggers off through the rolling, clunking train.

'I haven't been out in some nature for ages, years.'

'I don't see how you can avoid it in our town, Matthew. It's all around us.'

'Not if you live by the golf course.'

'I don't get you.'

I turn to her.

'The land's private round there.'

'Is it?'

She's never been down to his side of town. Her father probably plays golf there. I think it's sweet that she assumed everyone could use the parkland by his house.

'I'm afraid so. The view's OK though. We get the odd golf-ball as well. I used to sell them back to the clubhouse when I was a kid.'

'Very entrepreneurial of you.'

'Is that the hill?'

The train is chugging out of a cutting. Through a break in the trees I can see Saracen Hill jutting up into a very blue sky.

'That's it. We should ring a bell or something to make sure they stop.'

'I don't think that's necessary, Robbie.'

'I was kidding.'

The train slows and I can see the station, a tiny wood building and some benches standing back from the platform. Matthew steps over to the door and pushes it open.

'Ladies first.'

Sarah skips off the train. He turns to me in the doorway and smiles. It all seems to be working out.

134

The station is at the edge of the village. We leave
the building and walk up the main street. There
are some thatched cottages, a little village shop, a
pub and the restaurant Sarah was talking about.
This is a real chocolate-box English village.

'Quaint.'

'Don't you like it? Come on, Robbie, let's have a
look at the menu.'

We cross over to the restaurant window and
scan the menu board.

Matthew's behind us.

'I think we should get up there. She won't wait
long and it's almost ten.'

'Lead the way.'

I pull Sarah away from the window and start
chasing her up the street. She's laughing, pointing
out some of the features of the village as we get to
the outlying cottages. Matthew is marching ahead
of us but he still joins in with the banter. I've never
seen him chatting so much.

It starts getting very hot. We have to follow a
thin track with high hedges on either side then
cut across a field. There are insects buzzing
around, the morning sun is bringing out all the
wildlife. There are no clouds in the sky, just the
sun up in an endless blue. I'm sweating as we get
to the base of the hill and the incline gets more
acute. Sarah rolls the sleeves up on her T-shirt.
The grass is quite high, bits of it flick into my

face. My mouth is dry. Up ahead I can see the trees on top of the hill, swaying in a breeze.

'It looks cooler up there.'

Matthew is ahead of us, walking quickly, his goal in sight. I can just about make out a figure sitting under the trees. Sarah takes my hand and starts panting.

'Slow down, it's too hot.'

'I know what you mean. I'm sweating and we're not even half-way up.'

'Why don't you take your shirt off?'

'Yeah.'

I pull the Mambo T-shirt I'm wearing off my sweating skin and rest it on my shoulder.

'You should get a tan.'

'I don't get tanned. I get salmon pink.'

'You need a hanky for your head.'

'Very funny. Matthew, slow down, will you.'

He's way ahead of us. He flicks his head around then turns back to the hill without saying anything to us.

'He didn't look so happy.'

'No.'

Sarah understands quicker than I do.

'Maybe you should put your shirt back on.'

'Yeah, that must be it. I can't do it though, it would be even more of a dig.'

'Have you never seen him without a top on, in games lessons or something?'

'No. He was never around for games. He was taking extra exams or something. I guess they couldn't force him into the changing-rooms, considering he may have burns over the rest of his body.'

'But all that hiding away, Robbie. If he'd confronted you all in the first place, when you were younger, then it might not have been so bad.'

'I'm not sure younger kids would have been any more tolerant.'

'Maybe not but it's the fact he's always stood apart from everyone that's caused the problems.'

'You were getting on all right when we were on the train, weren't you?'

'Yes. He's much more relaxed when you're around though. It was a nightmare at the station before you got there.'

He's almost at the top now. I can see the figure is a girl, can see her walking towards him.

'Let's take it slowly. They can go round to the other side of the hill and we'll meet them later.'

'Sounds good to me.'

When we reach the top they're out of sight. Sarah flops down in the grass and I sit next to her. The horizon stretches off into the distance. From up here the fields are a patchwork broken by tiny roads and hedgerows far below us. The village and railway station are like an old-fashioned toy set they're so miniaturized. A breeze sweeps over us. I can hear the trees rustling behind me.

'This would be a great place for a party.'

She's lying back in the grass, stretched out in the sun.

'Why ruin it with a lot of people?'

'A party of our own then. Just the two of us. I wonder what they're talking about.'

'Probably the same things we are.'

'No, it's got to be more serious than that.'

She rolls over on to her stomach.

'I had no idea Cassie was into him. She's never been out with any of the guys at school. She spends most of her time criticizing them.'

'She may have a point.'

'It's quite romantic really, meeting out here.'

'They haven't got much choice.'

'So what's Matthew going to do? He can't run from Luke for ever.'

'He told me he'll stop running depending on what Cassie says.'

'A declaration of love.'

'Something like that. I see them. They're coming round.'

Matthew and Cassie are circling the hill. They're holding hands. Matthew's smiling, he looks at ease walking next to her. Cassie sits down on the grass.

'Hi, Sarah.'

'All right, Cassie, how are you?'

'Good. Are you two hungry? I've been standing out here for ages.'

'Robbie's going to treat us. There's a café in the village.'

'Will they be open yet?'

'I think it said eleven o'clock, so they should be by now. Otherwise we'll knock them out of bed.'

We stand up and start down the hill. Cassie and Sarah take the lead. I lag behind with Matthew.

'How'd it go?'

'Luke's been trying to turn her against me but she held on. We're going to make it happen.'

'Great. We should celebrate.'

'I'm going to have to see him.'

He looks happy but cautious at the same time. Things are working out for him but there's still a lot to do.

'I've been waiting for some encouragement from her. She wants to see me but she doesn't want to have to run away or hide from everyone. I think she's glad you two came by the way. Thanks.'

'We're enjoying the great outdoors, don't worry about it.'

'It almost feels normal, just being able to come out with a couple of friends, see Cassie. I can relax out here, there's no pressure, no one to hassle me.'

I remember London, the journey I took in the taxi.

'Wherever you go you have to deal with problems though, Matthew. You can keep moving around but eventually you have to settle, make friends, work, all that stuff. And it doesn't matter where you do it. People are the same everywhere.'

'You think I don't know that? I just mean for a

break. The town's too much at the moment. I know what I'm going to have to cope with in the long run, Robbie. But after I've seen Luke it'll be easier. He's the one who's causing the real hassle here.'

'And what exactly are you going to do about Luke?'

Matthew stops walking and turns to me.

'He'll call me out soon and I'll go and see him. I'll probably get a beating and after that I'll keep coming back and back until he has to realize that it's hopeless, that I won't give in to him. Even if Cassie had said she'd go tomorrow, move away, then I'd still face him. I want him to know I won't be told what to do, by anyone.'

'But he's dangerous.'

'I'm not running any more. Don't worry, I'm not going to drag you into this, more than I have done already anyway.'

'You haven't asked me for anything, except the meeting today.'

'I might ask you to come along if anything happens but not to fight for me. I've never had anyone before, just to be there with me, to show I'm not alone. You've been fighting Luke in a way, by supporting me. He's been trying to exploit the fact I'm isolated, using that to show that I'm somehow despicable. It makes me so angry. And the lies he's been telling . . .'

'I'm happy for you, that you got it together with Cassie.'

'You don't know what it means for me. Maybe in the autumn we can move, set up somewhere. I've got a study place . . .'

'I heard about it.'

'It won't be easy. We'll have to work and stay in some dive but that's like a dream for me, Robbie. I don't need much, just to be with her and to get away.'

'You'll do it. Come on, they're almost at the village. I have to stop Sarah from ordering a five-course special and bankrupting me.'

The 'restaurant' is a tea-shop with fancy cutlery. It's got the cottage-style low-beamed ceiling and a large fireplace with copper kettles and horseshoes. There's a picture of the Queen Mother on the wall above our table. We're the only people in there except a senile waitress and some grumpy white-haired guy back in the kitchen. They look surprised to see us. I put my shirt back on.

'The menu's a bit limited.'

Sarah puts on a Sloane accent as she studies and announces the list of crumpets, muffins and scones that comprise the lunch menu. I'm relieved to see the prices.

'Good, there's nothing over two pounds. I might have enough for the train fare back.'

Cassie sits next to Matthew, facing us across the table. I catch the look from the waitress when she sees Matthew. It doesn't alarm me any more, I've seen it a few times and I know he can deal with it. He's talking a lot, making some more of the joke remarks he was coming out with on the train. Nothing's going to get him down today.

'I'm going to have the house special and a magnum of champagne.'

'More like a muffin and a pot of tea.'

Sarah puts the menu down and looks across the table.

'How'd your exams go, Cassie?'

'I think I did all right. I froze in the last one, though.'

'Are you staying on?'

'I'm not sure yet. There's a chance I'll go down to London. With Matt.'

I haven't heard him called 'Matt' before. It suits him now, he's relaxed and playing around. All the tension seems to have come out of his body. His face is less strained as he smiles. I can imagine them together, their secret meetings by the bridge, a quick embrace and all the pressure draining out of him. With her he can let go, show all the elements of himself which he has to hide away from others.

Sarah picks up on Cassie's remark. 'Everyone's going to London. I don't see why everyone's so desperate to get out of the town. I hope you're not thinking of deserting me, Robbie?'

'I don't think so. I wouldn't be able to afford the phone bills, calling you every night.'

'Funny man! Seeing as you mentioned it, it's

partly the expense that puts me off moving. At least at university you get a grant.'

'How long's that going to last?'

'But you get some help. Until then I'm happy at home. It's cheap and all my friends are here.'

I feel like kicking her under the table. She knows that they're thinking of trying it in London. I don't deny her the right to an opinion but I'm surprised by her insensitivity. I look up at Matthew, expecting him to look uncomfortable with her words, but he's smiling.

'Not if they're all moving to London. Anyway, don't you fancy a change?'

'I'll get that at university. I'm not ready to move out yet.'

'Well, I'm sick of the school and the town. There's no point waiting around just because you're scared of making the break. I want a taste of the big bad city.'

'You could stay at Robbie's dad's flat. Now, that would be all right. If I had that place I wouldn't think twice about going.'

Matthew looks interested.

'Sorry, Matt . . .'

He smiles at my use of the abbreviation.

'My father's shipping off to the Orient and he's renting his place out. Otherwise I'm sure it would have been possible.'

'That's a shame. For you as well, if you're thinking of trying it there.'

Sarah answers for me. 'But he's not though. He's just pledged himself to my company.'

'I didn't rule it out completely.'

Cassie breaks in. 'The dragon's back. Stand to attention everyone.'

The waitress is shuffling over to our table with a grubby notebook. We give her the order and she creeps back to the kitchen. Cassie looks over at us.

'So what are you doing with the rest of the day? Do you want to try walking along to Redbury?'

It's another village a few miles away.

'I have to get back to town. Are you busy this afternoon, Sarah?'

'Ruth asked me round for a debriefing session.'

'Party gossip?'

'Apparently Ryan was really coming on to her.'

'Looks like we'll have to leave you to it, then. You don't look crushed to hear it.'

They look at each other.

'We're both keen walkers.'

'I see.'

The food arrives and there's a frenzy of teapots, strainers and sugar cubes being passed around. The dragon looks on in despair at the four of us chatting, munching and talking like any group of friends would do on a day out in the country.

We leave them in the village street, waving them off as they head up for the path to Redbury. The train is pulling in as we get on to the station platform and we climb aboard. Sarah says she's tired

144

after the lunch, so she lies out on the seat and rests her head on my chest. I sit by the window, watching the blur of green race by the train as we head for home. I'm still thinking about the way she was talking in the restaurant. I guess she thought it would be a pretence to try and soften her words, not to mention how happy she was at home and with her friends in the town. Matthew and Cassie didn't seem bothered. It was a good morning anyway. But I keep getting puzzled by Sarah. At times I can't think of anything I'd rather have in my life than to be with her but sometimes she seems very blunt, harsh even. The more I turn it over in my mind the more I realize I never knew her that well at school. She was like some kind of idol, the girl that every guy wanted to be seeing, the perfect girlfriend. All that's happened with Matthew has made me see some of the complexities of a relationship, the difficulties in really understanding someone. As long as I want to have a good time and take it easy, Sarah's the perfect companion. She's beautiful and intelligent, everyone likes her. But I want more than that. I was never one of the pure party guys. I've always been more broody than that. I didn't enjoy the party the other night, it's the same thing every time. I think that's one of the reasons she wanted to see me. Perhaps she saw that I was into other things than just hanging out in the town with the same faces for the rest of my life. But then she's putting me down for thinking about London.

It feels strange thinking like this. I was so happy with her yesterday, so content in the flat, away from everything else except her. But it wasn't real. It's not our flat. Like she said in the restaurant, if we moved up to London we'd be in a nasty little room, it would be tough. But Matthew and Cassie are prepared to try it. If you're that in love with someone then it can't matter where you are. Rooms are just walls and a roof, some furniture. The flat and the comfort it offers are important to Sarah though, it's part of the dream. I feel very young thinking about Matthew and Cassie trying it in London, a rented room somewhere in the endless suburbs of the city. Sarah and I will be hiding away in the dream flat, putting off the break from the town, if it ever comes. It was so good seeing Matthew and Cassie together, just enjoying each other, their freedom. That's how it should be, not the running around and the deception in the town. Sarah's sleeping, close to me. I can't stop thinking that we're going to have to face up to some kind of truth ourselves. I feel like I'm playing a part, that I was drawn to her by the way she looked. But I know I care for her. We'll work it out somehow.

The train rumbles into our town and stops at the station.

'Sarah, wake up. Home sweet home.'

'Huh? Are you going to walk me back then?'

'Sure.'

The streets are busy now, all the shops are full. Some of the pubs have their doors open and the drinkers are spilling on to the street, basking in the sunshine. There's a line of traffic on the high street, belching exhaust fumes into the air. Sarah goes into a newsagent's to buy a cold drink but she comes out because there's a long queue.

'It's bad enough here. Never mind London.'

'London's got a lot more than crowds and noise.'

'I've heard enough about how great London is today. The last time I was there I got stuck on a tube for half an hour, I lost my friends in Covent Garden and I got eyed up by a bunch of Italian guys in Soho who tried to buy me a coffee.'

'Sounds exotic.'

'I need a drink, really thirsty. I've had a muffin-overload.'

'Let's try in here.'

We go into a chemist's and she finds a fridge with some drinks.

'Want one?'

'No thanks.'

She comes out and joins me on the pavement, taps me on the arm.

'Hey!'

'What?'

She's got a juice carton in her other hand. She pushes it towards me and squeezes it, sending out a spray of purple liquid. I lean to the side and most of it misses me.

147

'Sarah, very amusing. I'm not a five-year-old, you know.'

'Oh, chill out, Robbie. You looked so moody I thought you deserved a shock. What's on your mind anyway?'

'Nothing.'

'Empty-headed again. Cheer up, will you? Hey, don't say anything, just kiss me.'

She reaches out and guides me to her lips. I don't know why I'm feeling so irritated with her. I put my arms around her.

'Sorry. I'm just being my usual pensive self.'

'I keep demanding your attention, Robbie. I can't help myself. Forgive me for being childish.'

'You're not.'

'All right then. Come on. I have to get back. Ruth will be coming around soon.'

We start down the high street. We take a few turns and we're on her street. Sarah stops outside her house and holds me.

'You're not still mad with me, are you?'

'Of course not.'

'I couldn't bear it if you were. I'm so worried about you meeting Luke as it is. Don't make me worry about how you feel about me.'

All her usual self-confidence is gone. She's almost pleading with me. But there's something about it I don't trust. She's overdoing it. I feel she's acting with me.

'I don't want you to stop caring, Robbie.'

'I won't. Stop it. This is crazy.'

I think she's going to start crying.

'I need you as much as Matthew does.'

'Sarah, what's got into you? Calm down. I'll see you tonight.'

'Call me when you've seen Luke. I'll be thinking about you.'

'I'll ring you.'

'I'd better go in.'

I kiss her and she moves up the driveway towards her door. I start walking off but turn to wave goodbye to her. She's out in the drive staring after me.

Chapter 7

As I open my back door the phone starts ringing in the kitchen. I think it's Luke, ringing to cancel, but when I lift it out of the wall holster I hear my father saying hello.

'Hi, Dad.'

'I was starting to think you'd moved out. I've tried a few times.'

'I know, I'm sorry. There's been a lot going on in the last day or two.'

'You know I'm leaving tomorrow?'

'No, I didn't. I've lost track of the days.'

'Flying first thing. Out of Heathrow.'

They'll be in business class. I can see him lifting a finger, demanding a newspaper and a brandy.

'When are you next back?'

'I'll be over in Europe on a business trip but I won't be back in England for some time. That's the whole idea, that I concentrate on the Pacific market. I'm handing the home market over.'

He goes on talking, telling me how he's restructured the company and got some 'new blood' in to 'run London for me'. I had been feeling guilty about not ringing him but as he goes on with the business spiel I lose interest. He can't say he's going to miss me or tell me he feels bad about leaving. The business talk is a protective screen for him.

'I'll be writing soon, Robbie.'

'I've never had a letter from you before. In fact, I don't think I've ever seen your handwriting.'

'It does happen but I'll probably dictate it. Otherwise it wouldn't be legible.'

So I get a neat note from the secretary.

'Best of luck with the results.'

'Thanks.'

'Have you decided what you're doing about college?'

'I don't know yet. I've been too busy to think about it.'

'What have you been doing? Girlfriend? I guessed you might be seeing someone the last time you were over. Your mother tells me nothing about you.'

'That and other things.'

'Send me a letter. I'm going to have to get off the line. It's bedlam round here. Sasha's having a nervous breakdown, last-minute stuff. Look, I'll see you soon.'

'Yeah.'

I feel as though he wants to say more. He's hesitant. But he's just waiting for me to give him the exit cue.

'Have a good flight, Dad. Send me your new address and I'll tell you all about it.'

'All right, Robbie. Look after yourself. Don't do anything I wouldn't.'

'Bye, Dad.'

He hangs up. I sit down and look around the kitchen. I'm in the middle for all these people: Sarah, Matthew, my father. I can't remember the last time I just kicked back with Ryan, did what I wanted to. I feel like I'm keeping everyone happy without having a thought for what I need. I stand up and go over to the fridge, pull out a tube of Coke. Then I amble through to the living-room and fall into a chair. There's a sound in the street, a harsh metallic scream. I jump up and stare out of the window. There's a car in front of my house, up on the pavement. Luke's standing next to it, leaning in through the window, pumping the horn.

I go out into the street. He's on his own. He looks better than the last few times I've seen him, almost smart in jeans, white trainers and a Hooch shirt.

'All right, Robbie. Let's take a ride.'

I open the passenger door of his car and roll in. It's an ancient Capri, very low on the ground. He fires the engine and rips into the street.

'Easy!'

The car's a wreck but the engine's tight. He flicks through the gears up to forty, takes the bend at the end of my street with a screech.

'I got it for a grand. You ever had a grand, Robbie?'

'No.'

'It feels good. You walk tall with a grand in your pocket.'

'A grand's a lot for this thing.'

I'm trying to sit up straight in a bucket sports seat. I have to shout at him over the engine noise. I want to make it clear we're on an equal level. I make my voice sound bold, as though I know something about cars and how much they cost, which I don't.

'I only turned seventeen a month ago, went out and got this. Don't judge by appearances, Robbie.'

We're already on the outskirts of the town. You can get out to the country in minutes. The road is thinning out, becoming a country lane, high hedgerows and a dirty brown tarmac.

'Watch this.'

He slips the gear stick back and the car lurches forward. I scan the speedometer curving upwards.

'It's got a tuned-up three-litre engine in it, faster than most things on the road.'

'I thought we were going to talk about Matthew.'

'We are. I'm taking you somewhere first though, got something to show you.'

He reaches down to the floor and picks up a gold-coloured pack of cigarettes. The floor of the car is covered in trash.

'Want one?'

'No.'

He fires it up, looking through the plumes of smoke with squinting eyes. The road is rushing towards us at sixty miles an hour. My left hand is gripping the base of my seat. All the muscles in my body are locked tight.

'I was really unhappy when I heard about you and Sarah seeing each other, Robbie.'

'Oh, yeah?'

'Should have been me, boy. I get on better with her than you do. I know what she's about.'

'She made her choice.'

'True. For now, anyway.'

He turns and smiles at me, the cigarette wedged between his lips. He must smoke like this a lot. I can see a brown smudge at the side of his face, a stain from the nicotine.

'I'm not here to talk about Sarah. If I was you've got nothing to say to me anyway.'

'Big talking, Robbie. A real bad man. You think you could deal with me, don't you?'

'I just want to hear about Matthew.'

'You think you'd last with me? And over this defect Matthew, that's what I don't understand. You've been with him, haven't you? I can smell him on you.'

'Why do you hate him so much?'

'Because he's like a cancer, trying to spread all the time, infecting you. Because he's warped, defective.'

'I don't know how you can think that.'

'You will soon.'

We're miles out of town. There's no other traffic, just us talking and the scream of the engine. All the windows are open in the car, the wind is whipping my face. The smoke from his cigarette is making me feel sick. He worries me. He's psychotic. There's a demented gleam in his eyes when he talks about Matthew.

'I'm going to measure him up. Measure him up and put him away, Robbie.'

He flicks the cigarette out of the window. I turn around and see it bounce down the road in spasms of red sparks.

'I'm wiser after a while in London, Robbie. I've seen how to get ahead. If you weren't such an easy touch I would have asked you in with me, to be my man in this town.'

'I don't want to know.'

'I'm making money. And you think you're doing all right? Hanging out with funny face? Incredible.'

We're coming around on a circle road that heads back to the south side of the town, doing eighty. Luke bends down and triggers a sound system. A hard house track starts vibrating my spine, the speakers are down in the floor. It's as loud as being in a club. He fires a cigarette, stares at me and bursts into laughter, the cigarette bobbing

156

between his lips. On my left I can see the golf course, people strolling with their clubs, chatting over a few holes. I feel so far away from them here in the car with Luke, a thousand miles from the easy security of my town, the golf clubs, the steady job in the city, the voices on the television telling you not to forget about your pension arrangements. Luke's broken away from that life. He's running wild. Although I think the guy's crazy I have to admit I'm getting a buzz from being in the car with him. It's like some kind of power, the last power open to the desperate, that of rejection. Luke has rejected all the conventions, gone off to London, bought a death-machine with a mighty stereo system. Luke doesn't care. He's wild. Sitting in the car, pushing ninety now, soaking up the house track, I can understand the appeal. But there are other things about Luke that I can't accept – his violence, his arrogance, his obsessive determination to ruin Matthew. Without those he might be all right, I might even get on with him, but he's twisted. I don't want to be like Luke.

We take a turn and enter the south side. I recognize the end of Matthew's street.

'We're not going to his house, are we?'

'Yeah.'

'We can't.'

'We're going to his house. His old house. The one he burnt down.'

We take a right turn and Luke slows the car, it rolls forward, I can see the houses ticking past, one by one, through his open window. It's the street Matthew wanted to avoid when we were walking up to the high street.

'This one.'

At first it looks like any of the other plain brick buildings. Then I see the boards on the windows, the steel front door, the black struts of the roof which survived the fire. The front of the house has a dirty smear running up one side, like the scar on Matthew's face.

'Let's go.'

He tumbles out of the car and walks over to the front of the house.

'Come on. Don't you want to see it or something?'

I get out of the car. The house stands apart from the others in the street. They have lawns and tidy wooden fences, cars pulled up in the driveways. Matthew's old house is barren. The front garden is a square of scorched earth, covered in rusting cans and plastic bags bulging with garbage.

'What did you mean? About him doing it?'

'You didn't know, did you? It was Matthew who started the fire.'

He walks around the side of the house to the back garden. Here the damage is more evident. Most of the rear wall is missing, bricks stand in crazy patterns in the wall. The interior is exposed.

I can see pools of water and broken bits of wood and machinery littering the bare floor.

'People use it as a dumping ground.'

He steps over what remains of the rear wall and into what would have been one of the living-rooms. I follow him. The house is silent, like a grave, with black walls, the odd strip of wallpaper clinging on. The floor is a tip: broken glass, bleached crisp packets, pages ripped from pornographic magazines. On a sheet of paper I catch sight of a woman's torso, the torn fragment of a smile and a bare breast.

'Some of the local kids use it as well. Come on.'

He goes into the hall and stands at the foot of a decaying set of stairs.

'I thought they would have knocked it down.'

'Not round here. Cheaper just to leave it.'

I'm finding it hard to breathe. There's no air in the house except a hot, stale stench. I can't believe this is where it happened. I hadn't imagined what his house would look like. I feel like a trespasser, crashing into Matthew's memories. I feel so stupid. There is so much more to the situation I've got involved in than I had thought possible.

'We're going up.'

'No, I've seen enough.'

'Don't bale out on me now, Robbie. Come on. Tread softly.'

He starts up the stairs, careful where to place his feet.

'One at a time.'

There is nothing supporting the stairs. The banister is missing. I can see the boards bend as he steps on them, black sticks mounted into the wall. I follow him.

The first room is not so badly damaged. There are signs that people have been here recently, a newspaper and an empty packet of cigarettes, some crushed butts. Then we go through to the second room. There's a hole in the centre of the floor, black and yellow around the edges, thick planks burnt through.

'This was his room.'

'How do you know so much?'

He turns and grins at me.

'Don't go through the back. There's nothing to hold you up but solid air. The floor fell through. That was their room, his parents'.'

He rummages in his shirt, finds a cigarette and lights it. Now he leers at me.

'Satisfied?'

'I want to get out.'

'Don't rush it on the stairs. They're not safe.'

I get down the stairs, step over the rear wall and stand in the garden looking up at the derelict house. Luke joins me.

'It doesn't prove anything.'

'You look sick.'

'I felt weird in there. I couldn't breathe.'

'They say a fire-house never loses its heat. It was weeks before you could touch the walls.'

'You were here?'

'Of course. I knew him, didn't I?'

I walk around to the front of the house and lean against his car. He strolls after me, smiling and blowing smoke through his nose.

'You don't like it, do you? I don't blame you. It's a scary house, boy. I've been in there at night.'

'You were living here back then?'

'We've always lived around here. I remember his family moving in, some scrawny brat he was. I didn't like him even then, Robbie. He was always hiding away from us, a mother's boy, running to her skirts. I never spoke with him. But I knew he was weird then, I tell you. Truth.'

'What happened?'

'I don't remember it that well. I was only about eleven or twelve. My parents were shouting a lot, everyone was out in the street. It was in the afternoon. The house was all lit up, smoke pouring out of it. By the time I got there, funny face and his mother were lying out in the garden. The father never came out. There was a lot of noise. I guess that's when the back wall fell in. People were talking about it for weeks.'

'But you don't know he did it then, do you? All you've done is shown me a burnt-down house.'

'What about these then?'

He reaches through the open window of the car

and springs the glove compartment. I can see a sheaf of papers. He pulls them out.

'I'm not just a pretty face, Robbie. I've been doing some research. When it happened I remember a lot of rumours, talk flying around the neighbourhood. As soon as I heard about Cassie and him I went down to the library in town and checked into the records. I don't see how you can argue with what I found.'

They're photocopies of pages from a newspaper. I can see a picture of the house, some columns of print.

'This one, check it.'

He passes me the front page of a local newspaper. I know the name. It's one of the free papers they stick through the door. My mother puts them straight into the bin. Underneath a picture of the house there's an article. It tells how Matthew admitted starting the fire to the police. He claimed it was an accident, that there was a pile of papers that caught fire in the kitchen and he didn't know how to stop it. He tried to warn his parents but they were upstairs and he couldn't get them to respond. The fire spread in seconds. His mother had forgiven him, said she understood it was an accident. Matthew's injuries were enough to convince the journalist that he was innocent of malice but there was to be an inquiry.

'What happened at the inquiry.'

'Accidental death. He got off. They didn't want

to break him up from his mother anyway, even if he'd confessed it was deliberate.'

'It's not proof.'

'Come on, Robbie, grow up. He was a screwed-up kid when he got here. From what I've heard, both his folks were heavy drinkers, you've seen his mother. You don't believe that stuff about the papers catching alight by accident, do you? Matthew's sick. He probably didn't want to kill them, just shake them a bit. Who knows what they were up to with him anyway? But fires don't just "start". Someone has to light them and whatever Matthew may be he's not stupid. Anyway, he admitted that it was him who did it, so he's responsible for his father's death. Everyone round here knew he'd done it on purpose but there was no one to say anything, was there? His mother went crazy straight afterwards. She was a bit mad before, apparently, but this tipped her right over. And there was nothing left of his father, he was practically cremated. And I'll tell you, you ask Matthew about it and you'll see, if you can get him to talk that is. He shows no regrets, you get me? He's not sorry about it. I spoke with him a bit later and he didn't seem that bothered. I was too young then, I didn't know that he'd started it. He's sick, dangerous.'

'Why didn't you say something before?'

'I only found the papers a while back. By that time he'd been seeing Cassie a while and she was falling for him. So, I decided to deal with it privately. If it hadn't been for him seeing Cassie I wouldn't have been nosing around in this stuff in the first place.'

I can hardly stand, my legs are trembling. I had faith in Matthew, I've been helping him. All the time I knew nothing about him, what he'd done.

'It's all right, Robbie, he takes people in. That's his trick. He needs to be put down before he does something like this again. I'm not having him with Cassie, no way.'

'I want to get home.'

'I'll drop you.'

'No, I'm going to walk. This is all crazy, I need some time to think, to think it all through.'

'He conned you, Robbie. He's been playing you along.'

'Maybe you're right.'

He takes the papers out of my hands and opens his door.

'You know I am. I'll see you later.'

'Yeah.'

He fires the car ignition and takes off. When the sound of the engine has faded there's silence in the street. I stare back at the burnt-out house. Matthew told me there was more than I knew about, he warned me not to get involved. I feel angry and sick, cheated somehow. The house is looming over me, a spot of black in a street that's overwise flooded with sunlight. I start walking for the high street. My face is burning, I'm close to tears.

I don't know where to go, I feel lost. It's as though I've stepped out of rhythm with the rest of the world, become destabilized somehow. I think of Sarah, maybe I should go straight round there and tell her everything I've seen, but she's with Ruth. I don't want to see anyone else. I'm not even sure I can face Sarah. All her doubts have been justified. When I think of Matthew walking away this morning with Cassie I feel a rush of anger. Luke was right all the time. And this whole mess wouldn't have started if I'd just kept going in the woods, looked straight ahead and kept walking. Maybe my father was right, maybe he could tell I was heading for a fall when he gave me that bit of advice on the phone – 'Don't do anything I wouldn't.' But my mother said Matthew was worth the effort to get to know. Surely she can't know the truth about him.

The streets are empty now, the shops have closed, the pubs are in a quiet period before the evening crowd arrives. I stagger towards my house. I'm cold inside. Have I been wrong about him all this time? But he was honest with me, he hinted there was more to find out. I'm confused and feel desperately lonely. When I need help I ask my mother for advice, she's who I turn to, but I think she's with Jeff tonight.

There's no one to go and see. My street is

suddenly in front of me. I reach the door and unlock it, slam it shut behind me. Then I take the stairs up to my room and collapse on the bed. My head is pounding. I can't get away from these thoughts, that he's cheated me all this time, throughout everything, all these things I've been doing for him. I stare at the ceiling of my room waiting for the hurt to pass, waiting until I can call Sarah and arrange to meet her. I want to be back in the flat with her, to escape from the outside world again. I want to hold her. It's a long time before I start feeling better and when I do I've put Matthew out of mind. I want to forget about him. I'm hoping I'll never see him again.

Chapter 8

I slept badly that night. I dreamt I was back in the fire-house, trapped in a room, struggling to breathe as the smoke streamed through the floorboards, came under the door and filled my lungs. I broke out of the dream and woke up with the sheets wrapped around me, covered in sweat. I've only had bad dreams two or three times in my life, back when my folks decided to separate. It took a long time for me to get back to sleep, to forget the house. When I wake up to the sunlight and noise of a new day I feel better, as though the worst is behind me. I get dressed and head down to the kitchen, grab some tea and a bowl of cereal. Someone pounds on the back door. Before I pull it open I hear him shout.

'Hey, Robbie. Wake up. Revenge is sweet.'

It's Ryan, looking fresh considering how early it is in the morning for him.

'Yeah, you almost found me in bed. Missed it by about five minutes.

'You slept late.'

'Yeah, I didn't sleep too good. How come you're up and about? Has the town had an earthquake or something?'

'My dad's taken a "long hard look at my lifestyle".'

He's mimicking his father's sonorous drawl. I start laughing.

'It's time for a bit of discipline, son. Some of your habits are causing a degree of concern. I realize the exams have been a stressful experience but nonetheless . . .'

'Stop it. You want some tea?'

'I'll take a coffee. I'm turning into a real Java junkie, can't get enough of the stuff.'

'So what are you doing for him, seriously?'

'He's got me helping with tasks and stuff around the house. Today I had to get up early to go shopping with him.'

'You're kidding.'

'No, the Saturday shop had to be done. The men of the house were given the job. The supermarkets open at nine now, the sadists. He's of the sad opinion that if we get there at nine there'll be no one about but of course all the fanatical shoppers are there already, revving their trolleys in anticipation.'

It's good to see him, it reminds me how long we've been friends, how I can rely on him to be consistent. He's trustworthy.

'So an hour up there and I'm too wide awake to sneak off to bed. Seeing as you're an early riser I thought I'd come round and entertain you.'

'Here's your coffee.'

'Cheers.'

I sit down at the table and start on the cereal.

'You met up with Luke yesterday, didn't you?'

'Yeah. He showed me Matthew's old house.'

'You mean it happened when he was in our town? I didn't know. What was it like?'

'A chamber of horrors. Best left alone. And that applies to Matthew as well.'

'Huh?'

'I've been dumb, Ryan. The guy's as warped as Luke's always made him out to be. He showed me some stuff that proved it but I don't really want to talk about it. It makes me feel like a sucker.'

'How were you to know? You always assume the best about people, that's all. I thought there was something about him that wasn't right, like he was keeping a secret from everyone.'

'You were right.'

'Like I never worked out why he looked after his mother.'

'You knew that?'

'Yeah, I saw them a few times out in town. She was using him like a crutch, ordering him about, you know.'

'Maybe he feels guilty for what he's done. But let's talk about something else. I don't want to think about him, he doesn't exist any more as far as I'm concerned.'

'Well, if Luke does some of the things he's been saying, Matthew's about to stop existing.'

'I'm not interested.'

'Something changed your mind in a big way. You were fighting his cause last time I saw you.'

'That was then . . .'

I need to change the subject, can feel myself slipping back into the mood I was in last night.

'What have you got planned for the day then?'

'Nothing much. I might buy a CD. You coming into town?'

'Maybe we should go into London. I need a buzz.'

'You not seeing Sarah?'

'I spoke with her last night and she said she was busy for the afternoon. I'm meeting up with her tonight.'

'That doesn't give us much time to go up to the metropolis then, does it? Is she seeing Ruth this afternoon?'

'Drop it, Ryan. The girl isn't interested. She goes for the football stars. Your IQ's way too high.'

'I thought we could do something as a foursome, give me a chance to have a few chats with her without any pressure, enchant her with my words of wisdom.'

'Really. They'd see through it in a second if I casually hassled Sarah to ask Ruth along and then presented you, as if by accident. We could get the eleven o'clock train and come back around three or four. What do you think?'

'Let's do it. Are we just going to roam about?'

'Yeah. I need some action to get all this business with Matthew off my mind.'

I'd asked Sarah to cancel her afternoon arrangements. I was desperate to see her but she said she couldn't get out of it. I was going to hang around the house all day, kill time, watch some TV, wait until she was free and then meet her at her house. We can wander round to the flat later. But going up to London with Ryan will make the afternoon fly by and that's what I need. I don't want to be sitting around brooding all day.

'We'll have to move it if you want to get the eleven.'

'Yeah, I've finished. I'll just get some shoes.'

A few minutes later we're trotting down the high street, hurrying for the train.

The West End of London is a world of noise and bright light, faces flashing by and distracting me, freeing me from all the events of the last week. We wander around the music stores, stop for coffee then drop into the amusement arcades around Chinatown. I can't remember the last time I was so relaxed, just hanging with Ryan and not worrying about anything. The hours rush past and soon we're on the train back. I feel refreshed, ready to see Sarah and start enjoying the summer again.

'I'm definitely moving down there this year.'

Ryan's leaning forward in his seat, waving his hands around in an attempt to indicate the importance of what he's saying.

'It's like a village where we live. I've been speaking with Andy and Pat, they're still into getting a house to rent.'

Andy and Pat are some guys from our year. I get on with them all right but I'm not sure if I'd want to live with them.

'What about a two-bedroom place?'

'Too expensive. Anyway, it's more fun if you've got a whole house to do what you want in.'

'How are you going to afford it?'

'My dad said he'd help with the rent if it was reasonable. I'll have to get a job but there are loads of them in London. I'd get to meet people that way as well.'

'I think it would be difficult.'

'You're just jealous. I know you'd go for it if it wasn't for Sarah.'

'That's not a bad reason though, is it? Anyway, the money's a problem for me, more than it is for you.'

'Your dad would help out, wouldn't he?'

'If he wasn't on another continent he might.'

'Whatever happens, you can still come down and stay. We'll have a sofa to crash on.'

He starts talking about all the adventures and opportunities that await him in the capital. I agree with him that it's the place to go to but I can wait if it means avoiding breaking up with Sarah. I'd like to go to uni eventually and I can always go to one in London. Then I'll get a grant and a loan to help with the expenses. London costs. I'd taken the last of the fifty with me and some other money I had stashed in my room and it's all gone. The money just gets sucked out of your pocket in London, there's so much to buy and you have to pay to get around. I'm used to walking everywhere but London's too vast for that. Ryan carries on with his excited London rant and I look out of the window. I can see the town coming up, the first buildings showing through the trees. I've got options, choices to make about my future here, but it feels as though I've come back to reality. I've been in a trance for the last week. What matters is enjoying life while I get a chance, making the most of it in my town, in London, wherever.

'You've got a while before you have to decide about it, Robbie. If you want to come in on the house let me know soon though.'

'The four of us in a house, with no rules of any kind. It could be an experience.'

'Absolutely. A fridge full of drink, wild parties . . .'

'Baked beans for breakfast, lunch and dinner, dirty washing everywhere . . .'

'Stop being down on it.'

'I was kidding, Ryan, I think it sounds great.'

'The only problem is the exam results. If they're

bad I'm going to get grief from my dad. He's not likely to fund the London expedition for me to do re-sits.'

'You don't know how you've done yet. You probably passed everything.'

'I'd better get back and do some more jobs round the house for him for the next few weeks, though. I have to keep him sweet.'

'Just get up before noon every day and you'll be fine.'

'There are some good parties coming up. Have you heard about Craig's eighteenth?'

'No.'

Craig is one of the footballs stars that hang around with Morgan. His parents are rich. I heard they've promised him a little sports car for his birthday.

'It's on a barge, up on the Thames. We cast off and float into the sunset. Then there are some others the next week. There's a lot going on this summer. It's going to be tough keeping up my morning appearances round the house.'

'If you get smashed the way you were the other night you haven't a hope.'

'It'll be fun finding out though.'

The train rolls into the station and we hop down to the platform.

'You going over to Sarah's right now?'

'No, I'm going to head back and grab a bite to eat first. I'll walk over with you.'

We talk about the afternoon in the capital and some of the things we're going to do with the rest of the summer. I'm even thinking about my father. Maybe I should write to him and plead for a ticket over to Singapore, that would be a real adventure. I leave Ryan at the end of my street and stroll over to my house. I'll be with Sarah in an hour or two and I can lie back in her arms and tell her everything that's going through my mind. There's nothing I want more at the moment than to be with her. I find my keys and push the door open. It's not double-locked so I know my mother's back.

'Mum, it's me.'

I walk through the hall and into the living-room. My mother's standing in the middle of the room smiling at me. Matthew's sitting in the armchair I was about to flop into. He's smiling too.

'Matthew was going to leave but I told him he could wait for you. I knew you'd be back soon. We've been having a chat.'

'Really.'

She looks as though she's accomplished something, brought her son together with one of her worthy causes. I haven't been angry with her for a long time, for years, but I am now. It was my mother who told me I should get to know him. She started this whole thing. Matthew looks at home in my chair. He's lost all the nervousness now. He thinks he's tricked me on to his side and he's come into my house, been chatting with my mother.

There are some tea-cups on the coffee table, a plate of biscuits. He's been here for hours.

'I'll let you two have some peace.'

She walks past me towards the kitchen and I'm left alone with him.

Matthew looks up at me with a grin.

'Where've you been?'

'Let's go up to my room.'

I turn and take the stairs. He follows behind me. When we get into my room I shut the door.

'First let me thank you for the other day. I know it was a hassle and I'm very grateful, Robbie. Everything's cool between Cassie and me now. We spent the whole day together and talked it all through.'

I can hardly bear to be in the same room with him. He doesn't notice the way I'm staring at him. He wanders over to the windows and carries on talking.

'But it does mean I have to face up to Luke. I'm not running away any more. That's why I came around.'

I was so calm after the day with Ryan. I thought everything was back to normal. I hadn't considered that I'd have to deal with Matthew as soon as this. I just wanted to forget about him, forget everything about him.

'Luke's called me out for tonight. He doesn't think I'll be coming but I will. He's using it as another chance to humiliate me, to say I'm a coward and a freak, but this time I'll be there. I'd like you to be there too, Robbie. I don't want you to fight for me. It's my business. But I told you how important it is for me to have someone who'll come along with me, to support me. It'll show them all that I'm not alone, that there is someone who cares enough to be there with me. And I don't care what happens but at least I'll have stood up to him. It's a first step in proving to him that I won't give up, that I can't be stopped. He's always hated me, I can't change that. But I can face him tonight and if I'm not alone it'll mean so much to me, Robbie. Can I depend on you to be there?'

Now he looks over at me, he sees the expression on my face for the first time since coming into my room. I can see the easy confidence slipping from his burnt distorted face, can see the fear coming back into his eyes.

'I don't want to see you again, Matthew, never again. I want you to leave and I want you to disappear. I don't care what happens to you. You've lied to me from the beginning. I was dumb to ever get involved with you.'

Now his face has gone back to the look I remember from school, the frightened eyes, the half-turn of his head to hide the scar that is etched into his skin. He is silent for a few seconds and when he speaks his voice is thin and nervous, not the bold speech of a minute ago.

'What's happened? Robbie, tell me. It was him, wasn't it?'

'He showed me your old house.'

'No. He took you there?' Matthew is almost howling, his voice full of pain. 'I knew he'd turn you around. I said that when it came to it you'd betray me.'

'It's the other way round. You lied to me. All this time I didn't know the truth.'

'And I suppose you think you know it now. A few words with Luke and you don't want to see me again – what about some faith in me?'

'Faith? You've been cheating me, using me, right since that day I saw you in the woods. I trusted you and all the time you were everything Luke said you were.'

'Then trust me now.'

'You started the fire, didn't you?'

I've been screaming at him, my voice ringing with the anger that I can feel welling up in me, but suddenly the room is silent. Matthew looks as though I've ripped the heart out from his chest. He seems crushed and beaten.

'He told you that? And you believed him? I thought you had faith in me, Robbie.'

'Try telling me the truth then. Don't deny it, that you did it. I read it in a newspaper cutting that Luke had copied from the library.'

'I thought you were different. But when you had to make the choice between believing in him or me, you thought of the burns on my face, didn't you? You weren't thinking about me, about the

178

things I've said to you and the person I am. You were thinking about the scar, as though it's some kind of evidence against me.'

Now he steps close to me. For a second I think he's lost control, that he'll strike me, but his face shows weakness and confusion.

'Why do I have to justify myself to you? You should have believed in me, not Luke. What chance do I have with this?'

He lifts a hand to the scar.

'It's not that, Matthew.'

'Yes, it is. You might kid yourself it's not but you're wrong. You're so easily convinced by Luke. If someone told you some lies about Ryan or another friend you wouldn't believe them straight away, would you? But I've got a symbol of it on my face and body. It doesn't wash off. It's with me for ever. And you didn't think twice before you made your mind up about me because of it.'

'That's not true.'

'I'm going. You don't want me here, do you?'

'No. I don't.'

He's close to tears, staring at me in disbelief.

'I was so wrong about you.'

Then he steps past me to the door and I hear him rush down the stairs and slam the back door behind him.

Chapter 9

I sit down on my bed and try to calm down. The encounter has got my nerves buzzing. I'm sweating and the room is unbearably hot, airless. I go over to the windows and push them open. At least it's finished, I don't have to see him again. I knew it was going to be tough. Despite the fact I've only seen him a few times this week I was starting to treat him as a friend. But it had to be done. There's some air coming into my room now and I turn back to my bed. My mother's standing in the doorway.

'What happened? What have you said to him?'

'You wouldn't understand, Mum.'

'I heard the yelling and I saw him running from the house. I want to know what's happened between you two. He looked as though you'd treated him terribly.'

She looks concerned and I can't help feeling a twinge of frustration that she's protecting Matthew rather than me.

'You don't want to know. It would shatter your cosy ideas about him.'

I lie down on my bed and shut my eyes. I want her to leave, need to be alone until I meet with Sarah.

'Matthew's been honest with me. I have no "cosy" ideas about him. I know all about him.'

'Really? So you know about the fire?'

'I do.'

I don't want to upset her but she's pushing me into a corner.

'You should be careful about recommending him as a decent friend to people, Mum. He's dangerous.'

'You're not making any sense to me, Robbie.'

'I know that Matthew started the fire. And his father was killed in it, so Matthew killed his own father. I've seen proof. He admitted starting it. In some paper.'

'Matthew didn't start it.'

'You're blind to him, Mum. I've seen an article written about it when it happened. Matthew confessed.'

'He only said those things to protect someone. I shouldn't be telling you this but I won't see you victimize Matthew because of his own decency. It was his mother who started the fire.'

'No. I don't believe you, he's lied to you.'

'She started the fire because her husband was leaving her. Even then she was drinking to try and cope with it. Matthew's told me the whole story and his mother has confirmed it to me.'

'Why did he say he did it?'

'Because he'd already lost his father. His mother was in no fit state to defend herself and Matthew couldn't stand the idea of losing her so he told the police that he started it, downstairs I think.'

'That's right.'

'But it was actually his mother who did it. She started the fire outside their bedroom while the man was sleeping. Matthew told me about the two of them, the things they did, and I have to tell you it was probably for the best that the house was destroyed and the man died. But Matthew still lost a father. He got the wounds on his face trying to open the door, to save him, as the stairs were burning. I don't think he would have left the house except he had to get his mother out when it got bad downstairs. The boy's a hero. And it doesn't stop there. Matthew knows the truth about his mother but he's been caring for her all this time, looking after her. He knows that it's because of her he's scarred and has no family but he's looked after her for years. He told me that because of your help he was seeing a girl now and they might move away. For the first time he's ready to make the break from his mother, who's slowly drinking herself to death. She's past anyone's help these days. And you've wrecked all that you'd achieved with him. He was so happy when he came here today, I hardly recognized him. Why didn't you talk with him about it, give him a chance to explain?'

'I tried. He didn't want to talk about it though. I thought he had nothing to say to me.'

'He was expecting more of you. Trust maybe.'

'Anyone would have thought what I did.'

'That's true sadly. He's had to live with that all this time.'

'I'm going after him.'

I leap up from the bed and start for the stairs.

'You won't catch him now.'

'He's fighting with Luke but I don't know where. He came round to ask for my help, my support.'

'Can you find out where they'll be? I'll get in touch with the police.'

'Sarah will know about it. I'll get over there.'

'Call her.'

'It'll be quicker if I see her face to face. I'll have to explain it to her.'

'Hurry, Robbie. Ring me as soon as you know anything.'

'I'll try. I'm going to find him, don't worry.'

It only takes me a few minutes to run through the woods and make it to her street. I rush up the drive and pound on the back door. Kate pulls it open for me.

'All right, you trying to break it down or something?'

'Sorry. I need to see Sarah in a hurry.'

'You'll get my dad going and you will be sorry.

She's up in her room.'

'Thanks.'

I climb the stairs and step into her bedroom. She's in a chair by the window, flicking through a magazine.

'You're early. Not that it's a problem. I have to give Ruth a call before we go out though.'

'Something's happened, Sarah.'

'Sit down, you look exhausted. What's the matter?'

She comes over and puts her arms around me. Her hair smells fresh. I just want to hold her and kiss her but there's no time.

'Matthew came to see me. So much has been going on.'

'You sounded confused yesterday, after you'd seen Luke. What was it you were going to tell me about that?'

'That was before I knew the truth.'

'Slow down, Robbie.'

'I gave up on Matthew. I abandoned him. Luke showed me some stuff which made me think Matthew had started the fire.'

'Matthew did?'

'Yeah, but it's not true. Matthew's been covering for his mother ever since then, that's all.'

'Matthew started it.'

She's not listening to me. She steps away from me and I can see she's deep in thought.

'Sarah, listen to me. There's no time for this.

I have to know where Luke and Matthew are meeting.'

'Why? Didn't he tell you? Luke said Matthew would come running to you for protection.'

'It's not protection. He didn't want that. What do you mean "Luke said" anyway? Why've you been listening to him? When was this?'

She's still not looking at me. I can see she's building up to something.

'I knew you were wrong about Matthew, all the time. I knew he was no good.'

'But he is.'

'He's nothing but a freak, Robbie. I tried to get on with him, for you, even made the effort during that nightmare day out with him and Cassie. But he's twisted. I knew he was lying to you.'

I can't believe it's her speaking. All the aggression and prejudice that I associate with Luke and his kind are present in her words.

'He should have gone to a special school or something. He's not fit to be around normal kids. You've seen the way he's been playing around with you.'

'I've heard enough. Why didn't you say something before?'

'I wanted to give him a chance because of you. But now we both know that he's evil.'

She steps across the room and puts her arms around me.

'Just forget about him. He's trying to pollute you. And you're far too special for that.'

'Get off me.'

I push her away. She comes forward again, surprised at my reaction.

'Robbie, you know I'm right about him.'

'I've told you that you're not. I know the truth now. I can't believe that you've hated him all this time.'

'We don't need him.'

She's trying to touch me, as though it'll be fine again if she can kiss me. It's not going to happen.

'I had my doubts about you, Sarah. You're very pretty but I thought there was more than that to you. Now I don't. I just got sucked in by the way you look, should have known better.'

'Robbie, why are you talking to me like this?'

'Because you're selfish and small-minded. You just want to hang with all the beautiful people in the safety of this little town. All that stuff about getting to know each other better – I can't believe we were stupid enough to think we had something.'

'You're wrong. We're perfect for each other. It's Matthew who's done this. He's the problem, like a rotten apple, everything he touches is tainted, the same way he is.'

'I can't listen to any more of this. At least I know what you're really like now. Tell me where they are, Sarah.'

'You've only just got here. Let Luke sort him out.'

'I need to know where they are. You don't get it, do you? You haven't listened to me. I'm going to find Matthew and help him. There are too many people like you who want to keep him down, either by attacking him or by ignoring him. I was feeling like that about him earlier today . . .'

'Good, you've seen what he's like at last.'

'But I was wrong and I'm prepared to accept that. I let him down again. That's the second time he's needed me and I've failed him. It's not going to happen again. So, I need to know where they are, Sarah.'

I take hold of her wrists and stare into her eyes. 'You know, don't you? Tell me.'

'It's too late anyway, Robbie, they were meeting ages ago. Forget about him.'

'Tell me, Sarah!'

'It won't make any difference. And what about us spending the evening together? You always run off to see him rather than stay with me.'

'Where?'

She sighs and looks down at the floor. I think she knows that she went too far with the attack on him, that she can't rescue it with me now.

'I can't understand how you missed them on the way down there. They're in the woods.'

I turn from her and move to the door.

'If you've got anything good in you then you'll ring my mother and tell her. She wants to help him too. I'm going up there now to try and stop it.'

'How can you stop Luke? He carries a knife, Robbie. He's crazy enough to use it.'

'I'm not letting Matthew face him alone. Not this time. Call my mother.'

'Are you coming back? I didn't mean all those things I said, they just came out, I was angry you were still thinking about him, that's all.'

'I haven't got the time to waste talking with you. Get to the phone.'

I rush down the stairs and sprint past Kate in the kitchen. Then I'm out in the street, heading for the wall of green that marks the beginning of the woods.

Back on Sarah's street there was still a twilight glow as the evening advanced but here in the woods the trees block out the sky and it takes a minute for my eyes to get used to the dark. As I push through the undergrowth, listening for shouts or some indication of where they might be, I start thinking clearly about what's happened in the last hour. I was too shocked by Matthew's presence when I arrived home to react calmly, and then the truth from my mother sent me reeling. I had to act, it was no good just mulling it over. And that in turn led me to the truth about Sarah. But I'm still not ready to sit down and work it all out in my head. I'm moving deeper into the wood, coming back to the place where I first saw him in trouble. Everything has moved round in a circle. If I'd helped him back then, I wouldn't be here now.

I think I knew I'd have to face the challenge eventually and now it's happening. Everything has been leading up to this moment.

I haven't been into the woods when they're covered in darkness for a long time, not since I was a kid, running home late from a friend's house. Then I would put my head down and run as quickly as I could, trying to escape whatever I thought might be lurking there, waiting for me in the dark. Now I'm seeking it out, not running away.

I'm sprinting now, pushing through the bushes and scraping against the trees. Matthew and Luke must have been out here for some time. I have to reach them before it's too late but there are no sounds in the wood to guide me. I pause for a few seconds, listening, then rush on to the next possible location. As the minutes tick by I'm getting more desperate. My breathing is loud and rapid, I'm covered in sweat. I might be too late. Luke's been bragging about what he's going to do. Maybe this time he'll go all the way, really hurt Matthew.

And it will be my fault.

I'm thinking of the few times we've met in the last week. So much has changed. Perhaps this was all meant to happen, to teach me what's valuable in people, to teach me that you have to make a stand and trust people. I'm never going to turn my back on him again. I remember his words, describing Cassie and the future he wants with her, the look in his eyes as he thought of her. He only wants what other people take for granted, he wants to be with the girl he cares for. My heart's pounding now, I can feel the blood racing in my legs. I have to get there, to protect him, to show him that he's not alone. I've failed him before but not now.

I'm getting close to the clearing. The sky above still has strips of light between the clouds and I can see the top of the monument quite clearly. However, as I look towards the bushes the light gets murky and the greens and browns begin to fuse into a stain of colour. Then I hear a voice, a thin confident snarl up in front. It's Luke. They must be by the monument itself. I've no time for scouting around or coming up with some strategy. I crash into the clearing, panting, terrified but determined to rescue my friend.

Luke is standing in the middle of a small circle of people. I recognize his two friends from London and some of the local kids I was at school with. His face is very white, laced with beads of sweat from the evening heat. In front of him Matthew is kneeling, his face terribly bruised. His eyes are closed. Luke towers above him. And then I see it. Held aloft in the night air, a short ugly knife, ready to come crashing down into my friend. I'm trying to move, to get between them, but I'm too far away. I can hear each second crawl slowly past with the beating of my own heart as I lift my feet and charge across the clearing. They haven't seen me, they're all staring at Matthew. Got to get there, got to stop it. All I can see is the knife beginning its descent, the steel glinting. I reach out to him, pushing out my arm, stretching, trying to reach him.

'Luke, no, please.'

I'm screaming but no one can hear me. It's as though I'm not there, watching it all from behind a thick wall of glass. I see the knife curving down towards him at a deadly speed. My fingers are so close, almost there, by his side, but the blade flashes past me and bites into my friend. Luke pulls it free and steps back as Matthew collapses in the dust with a crash. I'm too late.

I fall to the floor by his side and cradle his head in my arms. My eyes are stinging with tears. I'm howling, my whole body is shaking. Luke has taken him away from me, killed my friend.

And now Luke stares down and notices I am there, holding on to Matthew. He looks frightened, shocked. He can hardly believe what he has done himself. He backs away, trying to get to the trees, to escape. I'm standing, releasing Matthew to the earth floor of the woods. I walk towards Luke and my hands are flying at him in a rage. He can't hurt Matthew any more. I don't know what I'm doing, I'm sobbing and yelling. I want Luke to pay for this. He sinks under my blows, begs me to stop. Luke is nothing. He can only pick on those who are weak and alone. But then his friends are suddenly on me from behind, smashing their fists into me. I can't feel anything. Seeing this happen to Matthew was more painful than anything they can do to me. But I am driven to the ground by their kicks and punches. I see Luke rising from the ground, brave again now that his companions have come running. The strength is flooding from my body. I'm still thinking of those seconds when I was running across the clearing, trying to reach him. I can't think of anything else.

The last thing I see is Luke stepping closer to me, the knife a sparkle of steel buried in his fist. His eyes are glaring into mine. I'm trying to speak but my mouth is full of blood, I can't breathe properly because of it. He's moving closer, it's getting hard to think now, I want to sleep, to drift off somewhere far away from all this. My eyes are closing, I can see lights flashing and there's lots of noise, it's nearly over. This time I'm going with Matthew, by his side. I won't leave him now, not ever again. Then I sleep.

Chapter 10

My father's smiling at me. He's in a suit but his tie is pulled loose and he looks quite scruffy. It's strange seeing him wearing a crumpled suit.

'Hello, Robbie.'

I can see a large white room, high windows stretching along the wall opposite me.

'I'm in hospital?'

'That's right.'

'That's good news.'

'You think so? That's not what most people would say.'

'I thought I was dying.'

'You came close. The police got to you just in time.'

'The police? In the woods?'

'Your girlfriend called them as soon as you left her house but they had to search the woods and it took them a while to find you. She's outside.'

'Sarah?'

'Yes. I've been talking with her. She's explained everything that happened. I'm very proud of you,

Robbie, for what you did.'

'I don't want to see her. You're proud of me?'

'For helping your friend.'

'I wasn't much help to him in the end, was I? I got there too late.'

My father takes my hand. It feels odd for a second, this intimacy between us, but then I feel a wave of relief that he's here with me. He wants to say something, comfort me even though I failed Matthew.

'He's alive, Robbie. You were both in a terrible state when they brought you in, he was a bit worse than you but he pulled through the surgery. He's going to be all right.'

At first I think he's just saying it to make me feel better, but he nods his head and I know it's the truth.

'But the knife?'

'He was badly hurt but he's tough. He's fine.'

It takes some time before I can speak with my father. My mind is alive with thoughts of the woods and the image of the knife rushing towards Matthew. But he survived. I feel like I've been given another chance.

'Maybe it's because he saw you that he hung on. I think that was important to him, that you came to help.'

'He saw me?'

'Yes. I've spoken with him.'

'He's here?'

'In another part of the hospital.'

'I want to see him.'

The thought that Matthew is still alive is all I can think of.

'There's lots of time for that later. You're not exactly fully recovered yet, are you?'

And now it's sinking in that my father is here by my side.

'You didn't go to the East then? You were still in London? I thought you'd gone.'

'I did go. But I came back when your mother rang me.'

'I don't understand. It was only last night.'

'No, it was four days ago. You've been unconscious all that time. We thought we might lose you for a while there.'

Even though he's smiling I can see the worry and fatigue in his face. He looks a lot older than he did the last time I saw him.

'Why didn't you tell me what was going on when you came down to London, Robbie?'

'There wasn't much to say. I didn't know for sure what was going to happen. Where's Mum?'

'She's outside. Do you want me to get her for you?'

He stands up and leaves the room. I can hear voices from beyond the doors then my mother comes in.

'Robbie. It's good to see you awake. You've been sleeping for so long.'

Her eyes are swollen and red. She presses her hands to my face.

'So good to see you.'

'You too, Mum. How's Matthew?'

'He's fine, worried about you of course.'

'What happened out there?'

'I'll tell you later. The doctors want to see you, they have to ask you a few things.'

'I'm still tired.'

'Then rest. We'll be here when you wake up again.'

My whole body is starting to ache. I want to drift back to sleep.

'Get me home as soon as you can. I don't want to stay in here.'

'I will. Don't worry, I'm here for you.'

I spent another week in bed, following the doctor's wishes. At least I was back at my house. I had a procession of visitors. My mother nursed me with tea and soup. Ryan made a daily appearance and tried to make me laugh. My father had to go back to town and fly out to the East after a few days but it meant a lot to me, him being there when I woke up. He'd been sleeping at the hospital, waiting for me to come round. I've already written him a letter, thanking him, telling him I'll be out there for a holiday to recuperate. Sarah came around a few times but I didn't want to see her. I've had time to think and I know we're not right for each other, it was nothing but a joke relationship. I want to get back to how it was before, with her as a casual friend, nothing more. Even that could be difficult, after what she said. We'll never be close. She's explained to my mother how she was wrong about Matthew and that it was some kind of jealousy that made her say those things about him. My mother understands it, she's argued her case. But there was really nothing between us. I was more interested in the way she looks than what was going on in her mind and when I finally saw what was there I knew we couldn't be together. I think she might have been hanging around with Luke all the time we were seeing each other anyway. It doesn't really bother me. I'm better off without her.

Ryan told me what happened in the woods. As usual he had the whole story first. Two policemen eventually found the clearing and saw me passing out under the blows from Luke and his friend. They stopped Luke just before he used the knife on me. They arrested him and he's coming up for trial in a few weeks, for assault with a deadly weapon on Matthew and me. People are saying he'll go to prison for years. I won't miss him. It was touch and go when they got Matthew to the hospital.

I'm much better now, well enough to visit him every day on the ward. The first time I saw him I realized there was a real bond between us, we didn't have to say much. Now we talk for hours. I know everything about his childhood, his parents, the fire and the way he's coped with it ever since. Everything my mother told me was true. I should never have doubted him.

He went to the woods on his own after seeing me that night, let down by the only friend he thought he had. He had to stand in a circle of onlookers and take the abuse from Luke. All because he wants to be with Cassie and he has to fight for the things he wants in life. Matthew is the bravest person I've ever met. I feel lucky to know him. He doesn't want sympathy or charity from people. He just asks for the same respect that he shows to others. He's so happy with Cassie now. She comes in to the hospital all the time and when he gets out they're going down to London to give it a go away from the town, making a fresh start. I'll be visiting them. I might even make the break and move down there myself in the autumn but I'm not sure yet. I need some time to relax and think things through.

I've learnt so much from Matthew. He's had so many disadvantages but he's triumphed in the end, because of his determination and strength of character. He told me that when he heard my shout in the wood he knew it was going to be all right, even though he was badly wounded and could see the knife coming. That's when he knew he was going to make it. He said he didn't want to lose everything he'd hoped for, he wasn't going to let it be taken away from him. Not only would he have lost Cassie if he'd given up the fight for life, he would have lost a true friend as well. We'll always be there for each other now. Like blood brothers. I'll never forget this summer.

Don't miss out on other Tear Jerkers books:

Runaway
Once in a Blue Moon
Family Secrets
Remember Me
Second Best

SAPLING ORDER FORM

NON-FICTION

0 7522 0247 2	StarFiles	£4.99 pb

TEAR JERKERS

0 7522 0246 4	Family Secrets	£2.99 pb
0 7522 0251 0	Once in a Blue Moon	£2.99 pb
0 7522 0241 3	Remember Me	£2.99 pb
0 7522 0236 7	Runaway	£2.99 pb
0 7522 2220 1	Second Best	£3.50 pb

CALIFORNIA DREAMS

0 7522 0906 X	Perfect Harmony	£3.50 pb
0 7522 0916 7	Playing for Keeps	£3.50 pb
0 7522 0911 6	Who Can You Trust	£3.50 pb

HOLLYOAKS

0 7522 0145 X	Coming Together	£3.99 pb
0 7522 0150 6	Can't Get the Girl	£3.99 pb
0 7522 0155 7	New Friends	£3.99 pb

0 7522 0296 0	Independence Day: Junior Novel	£3.99 pb

0 7522 2240 6	It Takes Two	£3.50 pb

SAVED BY THE BELL

0 7522 0623 0	Bayside Madness	£3.50 pb
0 7522 0618 4	California Scheming	£3.50 pb
0 7522 0196 4	Computer Confusion	£3.50 pb
0 7522 0191 3	Don't Tell a Soul	£3.50 pb
0 7522 0901 9	Girl's Night Out	£3.50 pb
0 7522 0181 6	Impeach Screech	£3.50 pb
0 7522 0608 7	Kelly's Hero	£3.50 pb
0 7522 0613 3	Ol Zack Magic	£3.50 pb
0 7522 0995 7	One Wild Weekend	£3.50 pb
0 7522 0186 7	Silver Spurs	£3.50 pb
0 7522 0990 6	Zack's Last Scam	£3.50 pb
0 7522 0985 X	Zack Strikes Back	£3.50 pb

SAVED BY THE BELL: NEW CLASS

0 7522 0670 2	Breaking the Rules	£3.50 pb
0 7522 0665 6	Going, Going, Gone	£3.50 pb
0 7522 0660 5	Spilling the Beans	£3.50 pb
0 7522 0655 9	Trouble Ahead	£3.50 pb

STORY STORE

0 7522 0159 X	Quiet Day	£3.50 pb
0 7522 0164 6	Helping Hands	£3.50 pb
0 7522 0169 7	Special Delivery	£3.50 pb
0 7522 0174 3	Who's Minding the Store?	£3.50 pb

0 7522 1041 6	Testament	£14.99 hb

TOMORROW PEOPLE

0 7522 0637 0	The Culex Experiment	£3.99 pb
0 7522 0652 4	The Living Stones	£3.99 pb
0 7522 0642 7	Monsoon Man	£3.99 pb
0 7522 0647 8	Rameses Connection	£3.99 pb

TOMORROW'S WORLD

0 7522 1603 1	Environment	£4.99 pb
0 7522 1691 0	Genetics	£4.99 pb
1 85283 337 8	Medical Genetics	£9.99 hb
1 85283 334 3	Space	£9.99 hb
0 7522 1686 4	Space	£4.99 pb
0 7522 1608 2	Transport	£4.99 pb

1 85283 386 6	Zig and Zag: In Yer Face	£4.99 pb

BUG FILES

0 7522 0323 1	Shock Roach	£2.99 pb
0 7522 0313 4	Squirmsters	£2.99 pb
0 7522 0328 2	Mut-Ants	£2.99 pb
0 7522 0318 5	Tyrantula	£2.99 pb

0 7522 0347 9	Masked Rider	£3.50 pb

*All these books are available at your local bookshop or can be ordered direct
from the publisher. Just tick the titles you want and fill in the form below.*

Prices and availability subject to change without notice.

Boxtree Cash Sales, P.O. Box 11, Falmouth, Cornwall TR10 9EN

Please send a cheque or postal order for the value of the book and add the
following for postage and packing:

U.K. including B.F.P.O. – £1.00 for one book plus 50p for the second book, and
30p for each additional book ordered up to a £3.00 maximum.

Overseas including Eire – £2.00 for the first book plus £1.00 for the second
book, and 50p for each additional book ordered.

OR please debit this amount from my Access/Visa Card (delete as
appropriate).

Card Number ☐☐☐☐☐☐☐☐☐☐☐☐☐☐☐☐☐☐☐☐

Amount £ ....

Expiry Date ....

Signed ....

Name ....

Address ....

....

....